To Wen...

C000182545

Angel

Wendy Beasley

Angel

Wendy
Beasley

Victorina Press
www.victorinapress.com

Typesetting and layout: Jorge Vasquez
Cover design: Triona Walsh

British Library Cataloguing in Publication Data
A catalogue record for this book is available from the
British Library.

ISBN: 978-19169057-7-1

Typeset in 11pt Garamond
Printed and bound in Great Britain by 4edge Ltd

Chapter 1

I heard the key in the lock and pretended to be asleep; I closed my eyes tightly, held my breath, stayed silent and kept absolutely still. I looked at the baby, fast asleep in his cot next to the bed, and felt a moment of terror. He mustn't wake, he mustn't cry, nothing must make his father angry.

'Lydia, get in here now!'

It was strange how hearing my own name filled me with so much dread. I could remember being secretly pleased when, as a little girl, I realised someone who loved me had given me that name. It didn't matter why they'd given me up or let me be taken from them, they'd spent time picking a name which was both beautiful and quite unusual. So they must have loved me, if only for a short while. Yet the sound of my name on Leo's lips filled me with terror.

I'd long since given up trying to work out what I might have done to displease him, as I knew it needn't be anything real. It could be an imagined fault or instance of neglect of which I was totally unaware, and it was useless trying to apologise. That just made things worse. There was no point pretending not to hear, no point in delaying and fuelling his anger, as then he would come and find me, and I didn't want to risk him waking the baby.

I turned back the covers and climbed out of bed, felt a twinge in my shoulder from the last time this scene had played out – only the previous day. I moved slowly towards the bedroom door, desperately trying not to wake the baby, wondering once again if this would be the last time. Recently, Leo had added a new element to each onslaught of abuse; partial strangulation was now the finale. The last time it happened I silently willed him to get on with it, to finish it once and for all. Yet I was quickly overcome with guilt when I thought of my innocent baby boy, so I fought hard to stay alive for him. But now it was going to happen again, and there was nothing I could do to stop it. I walked through the door towards him, and towards the pain and humiliation which awaited me.

***

The beating which followed was no better, no worse than any of the others, so I've no idea why that particular incident on that particular night was the catalyst which brought about my decision to leave. Lord knows I'd had reason enough for a very long time, even before the baby was born. There was the beating I endured for getting pregnant, followed by numerous attempts to "get rid of it", culminating in the battering the night before he was born. Medical staff believed the story of a head over heels fall down the stairs, and it was easier to let them believe it in the face of Leo's constant presence and feigned concern. I can still feel the almost unimaginable pain of that night when my poor baby boy took his first breath. By some miracle he clung on to life, yet I was gripped with fear, wondering what would happen to us both.

Things didn't improve when I brought the baby home. After one restless night, Leo told me I would have to move the boy to another room as he was disturbing him. I said I would sleep out there with him, but was told my place was in bed with my husband. Somehow I persuaded Leo to let the baby stay with us, but I would leap up at the slightest sound and take him out of the bedroom.

I don't think he was a particularly difficult baby, although I had nothing to compare him with. He would wake, cry, feed and then go back to sleep. As far as I could tell, that was what babies did. I didn't know any other mothers or belong to a mother and baby group, so I was very much working on instinct. Yet other than his father's complaints I was sure things were progressing normally.

However, the constant ridiculing of my attempts at motherhood undermined my confidence, ensuring permanent feelings of inadequacy. I thought the beatings might stop after the baby was born, and really hoped Leo would develop some kind of fatherly love and concern for his son. I have no idea why I was so hopeful, but I couldn't have been more wrong. Only a few days after the birth, the crying baby in my arms drove Leo to such anger that he tried to wrench him from me, only stopping when I dropped to my knees to shield him. He resorted to kicking me instead, and I was so afraid one of his kicks would connect with the baby I almost smothered him in my attempts to keep him safe. It was clear the baby had changed things, yet sadly not for the better; now I knew without doubt that both of us were in danger.

The sex, which always followed a beating, was another form of abuse. It could go in one of two directions: a punishment rape to inflict even more pain and humiliation than the preceding battering, or, very occasionally, I was treated to snivelling apologies and declarations of undying love. Lately the former had taken precedence. Both sickened me beyond belief, but I could see no alternative other than to endure, desperately hoping neither type of coupling would result in another pregnancy, which I could do nothing to prevent. I was never allowed out to visit the doctor or a family planning clinic, so there was no chance of going on the pill, and yet should I fall pregnant again it would be deemed entirely my fault, and I must expect to be beaten for it.

So I can't say for sure why this almost everyday occurrence brought me to the momentous decision I'd spent so long avoiding. Of course I'd thought about it before, but unfortunately not until after I found myself pregnant. Up until that point, although Leo could be surly and demanding, he was never violent, and I was still naïve enough to think

I could do something to get back the Leo I'd fallen in love with. The optimistic part of me believed it would all work out somehow, and I couldn't see that everything was leading inexorably towards him taking total control of my life. Now I knew that if things continued as they were he would eventually kill me, and leaving was my only chance of survival. I knew I had to overcome all the familiar negative arguments that formed in my mind. Where would I go? What would I live on? How could I support the baby on my own?

I'd never known the love I felt for this small human being, and when his father wasn't there our time together was so precious. He'd started to truly smile, focussing on my face with his huge blue eyes – which could only have come from me – gurgling and smiling and making me proud. I could see nothing of his father's darkness in him, he was pink and round and perfect in every way. Despite Leo making me feel I wasn't good enough, when I was alone with my son I felt like a proper mother, and knew I would do anything for my precious baby boy. So perhaps I could leave, perhaps I could start again and give him the life he deserved.

The following morning I dared to start planning, but as I plotted my escape, my mind kept drifting back. Where had it all gone wrong?

***

When Leo walked into my life he was handsome, clever, a brilliant sportsman – an irresistible combination to the naïve university student I was then. Flattered by his attention, I found it hard to believe that this gorgeous man all the girls were drooling over could be interested in me, yet it seemed he was. His intense gaze took my breath away, and when he asked me to go for a drink I was thrilled to accept. He was in his third year of an education degree, though unlike me, who simply wanted to teach, he saw himself as a head teacher, and eventually as a part of Ofsted or some other governing body.

Back in those days I was in awe of his ambition, I didn't see it as anything more ominous than a tremendous desire to do well. However, in reality, it was another example of his need for power. He would never have been happy being told what to do, and he hated being criticised in any way, so he'd set his sights on being the one giving the orders and finding the faults.

Getting a place at university had been quite an achievement for me after all the foster homes which didn't work out and the placements in assorted children's homes. I became well used to rejection, but the one constant in my life was a love of learning. Even changing schools several times didn't dampen my enthusiasm, and I was often a pleasant surprise to the teachers, who expected nothing and were amazed by what I produced. Had I been a normal child, living with normal parents, they might have recognised how bright I was, but with my disjointed and disrupted home life there was very little opportunity to find out what I was truly capable of. Even without encouragement I was smart enough to realise that the only one who could help me was myself.

By the time I was fifteen I'd been placed in my final foster home, which turned out to be the best I'd ever known. Sheila and Terry Grant were a kind and loving couple who took a real interest in my school work, which no one else had done. I was only supposed to be there for a year and then expected to make my own way in life. By then I'd decided I wanted to be a teacher, and they were the first people I told. I explained I needed to go to university and that it wouldn't be easy. They encouraged me to follow my dreams and told me I could stay with them for as long as I needed, promising that if I stayed on at school and studied hard to get the grades then they'd give me all the help they could. True to their word they set me up with a laptop, bought the required books, encouraged me with my studying and exam revision. They liaised with the school to see what help I needed, just as proper parents would, and for the three years I was with them that's exactly what Terry and Sheila were. I don't think they received any allowances for me after the age of sixteen, so everything they did for me was down to their own generosity, which made me even more determined to get to university and reward their faith in me.

Deep down I was sure I could do it; I worked very hard, both at school and in all manner of part time jobs, keeping all the money I earned for driving lessons and to save up for my own car. Once again Terry and Sheila helped me, finding me an old but serviceable Micra, even putting some money towards it for me. When the little blue car came into my life it was my pride and joy.

That was the the beginning of my longed-for future, and what a magical beginning it was. When the time came to decide where I would do my degree, the University of Brighton was at the top of my list. Brighton was rated as outstanding by Ofsted but their entry requirements were quite high, so I would need grades at least as good as predicted. I was determined to make this achievable but – just in case – I put the University of East Anglia as my second choice. This was in Norwich, much closer to my present home in Norfolk, and I received an unconditional offer from them, so at least it was certain I'd be going to university. The UEA was a good university, but somehow it didn't seem as exciting as the idea of going to Brighton. In those heady days I was only interested in the best, so I worked very hard to reach the standard they required, and was thrilled to get the grades which guaranteed my first choice.

When the time came, with no barriers in the way of my ambition, my resolve deserted me. Who did I think I was? Kids from care like me didn't go to university, and although I had the grades and I'd been accepted, it still felt like an improbable dream. So far, virtually nothing in my life had been reliable, and my present foster carers were the only ones who hadn't let me down. I had never been ill-treated, starved or beaten and – judging from the tales I heard from some other kids in care – that was a bonus. Lots of people had been kind, and there had always been genuine concern for my welfare; however, I had never known unconditional love.

I hadn't given anyone any trouble in my short life, nor had I complained when I was moved from place to place to make way for more needy kids. Though I'd soon learned that people – both adults and children – didn't hang around for long. Social workers left or were promoted, kids were moved without any rhyme or reason, and foster parents were oversubscribed, so children in the greatest need always came first. I was never one of these; I was just good old Lydia who didn't make a fuss and went where she was put without any argument.

Sometimes I wondered about my real parents – for I must have had real parents: a mother and a father. So where did they go? I was never told, and could only ever remember being in a children's home or with foster parents. I had no idea how or why I'd ended up in care, and I was resigned to the fact that I'd probably never know. I imagined a number of scenarios: a mother who died in childbirth and a father who died of grief; a mother and father who died together in some freak accident. Somehow I couldn't face the fact that my parents were still alive, for that meant they simply didn't want me. My imaginary parents changed each time I thought about them: from very rich professionals to farmers; from British to deposed foreign royalty – although the latter seemed unlikely as there was nothing in any way foreign about me.

I'd been with Sheila and Terry longer than with any other foster parents – in fact longer than in any other place – so it was the nearest thing to a home I'd ever known. When the time came to say goodbye it felt worse than any of my previous moves, but in the end it was just moving on again, something I'd learned to accept a long time ago. As I packed my few belongings into the Micra and said my farewells, I was sad to think I may never see this lovely couple again. They were the nearest thing to parents I'd ever known, and I was close to tears when they told me I could come back at any time, and that, if I didn't like uni, there would always be a home for me with them.

It was a very long drive to Brighton and, having not long passed my test, quite a scary one too; a baptism of fire in the way of experience. Once I'd arrived at the university campus I felt I could drive anywhere.

I soon found my allotted lodgings and discovered I was one of six students sharing. There were two other girls and three boys. We each had our own room but shared a bathroom and a kitchen. That didn't bother me as I was quite used to sharing – I'd done it all my life. I'd also learned how to instantly fit in with others, so I dropped into my 'new kid in the children's home' routine and soon got to know them. Two of the boys were from abroad: Choy from Hong Kong and Dusan from the Czech Republic, while the other boy, Will, was a Brightonian, so hadn't come far at all. The two girls, Amy from Surrey and Emily from Northumberland, both seemed very friendly.

The thing which first struck me about the Falmer campus was the glorious light. There was an abundance of glass in every part of every building, and light flooded in. The restaurant, library, science labs, art rooms and lecture theatres were all bright and modern, yet welcoming and comfortable; a combination difficult to achieve. From the moment I arrived I felt at home. Despite taking days to find my way around and spending my first week in a state of bewilderment, I loved it, and knew I'd done the right thing. I enjoyed everything about university life: the shared accommodation where I learned to cook; the lectures which filled my days with the joy of learning; the social life which filled my nights with fun. At last I had found somewhere I fitted in, and I wasn't judged by my background. No one was interested in that, it was all about who I was today, and that suited me fine.

I fell in love with Brighton too. The Lanes provided a shopping experience like no other, and the Royal Pavilion and gardens were breathtaking. I went to my first live concert at the Dome theatre, and soon decided this was the city I wanted to live in for the rest of my life. I forgot all about my previous life: the heartbreaking moves, the rejections, and even – to my shame – Sheila and Terry. I had come home.

The lecturers were encouraging and were pleased with my work, and I was beginning to make real friends for the first time in my life; I'd never stayed anywhere long enough to make lasting friends before. Amy was my best friend and we spent most of our free time together. She was very funny and the complete opposite of me, bubbling with confidence and a member of a large, loving family who were constantly messaging her and sending her news from home. Our shared accommodation meant we frequently talked long into the night about our feelings, hopes and dreams. After my rocky beginnings I'd really found my feet. I began to glow with a new-found confidence – which had no doubt rubbed off from Amy – and looking back, I think that's what attracted Leo. I was a challenge he had to conquer, a confident young woman he had to possess. He was too sure of himself, too wrapped up in his own importance, to see how fragile I really was – or perhaps that's what he wanted, someone who wouldn't put up much of a fight. I was surprised by Amy's reaction to him, concerned she felt he wasn't to be trusted, yet although I usually took notice of her opinions I couldn't see any reason to worry.

Unlike Amy, who always reminded me of a film star with her long blonde hair and perfect figure, I was never a beauty. Taller than average, thin and angular, with mousy hair and long limbs, back then I looked more like an athlete than a star of the screen. However, I started to experiment with makeup and added a few blonde highlights to my hair, so with my blue eyes – which were my best feature, even under my own harsh scrutiny – I looked okay. There were boyfriends, but mostly they were just that: friends who were boys. There were a couple who took me out or made up a foursome, but nothing serious. Until I met Leo.

Chapter 2

Leo was a friend of Will's, and it was Will who introduced us. I soon discovered that although everyone called him Leo, his full name was Leonid Kolocov. He told me proudly that the meaning of Leonid was lion, and as this was also associated with the more common name of Leo, he was happy with the shortened version. I remember finding it quite endearing; his delight in the meaning of his own name was almost childlike. He was from Russia, which surprised me, as he spoke almost perfect English, but he explained that his mother was English and had always insisted he spoke her mother tongue correctly. His family were all still in Russia, though he never elaborated. I learned nothing about them at all, yet as an orphan this didn't seem strange to me. So when he said he'd like to take me to meet them, I was foolishly happy at what appeared to be some kind of commitment, and I started to dream of our future together.

And so it was that Leo came into my life, and although I couldn't have known then, it was also the start of my downward spiral into despair.

I was ridiculously optimistic in those days and there were no clouds on my horizon. I had overcome all obstacles to get to university, and there was nothing I couldn't do. I was flattered by Leo's interest but also unwisely over-confident. I started to believe I deserved the attention of this wonderful man and was far more attractive and exciting than I'd previously realised.

I've often asked myself if there was anything to warn me of what was to come. How did I fall so easily and not see the man behind the mask? I've pondered on what I could have missed, but can only remember him being charming and attentive.

Except for the girl. The one he said was unbalanced, who appeared to me to be extremely distressed. She turned up on campus one day, shouting and screaming at Leo. It was clear from the crowd which had gathered around them that some sort of scene was in progress, but I was too far away to hear what she was saying. It was obvious from her body language she was very distraught, and it made me slightly uneasy to note how she pulled back as if in fear when Leo took a step towards her. By the time I reached them she was running away, and the crowd had started to disperse, but I did notice that everyone looked uncomfortable, and even those I knew wouldn't meet my gaze. When I asked Leo about her he said she was a girl he'd known in his first year, who'd got herself pregnant and tried to blame him. He said she'd lost the baby, and it had left her unbalanced, and now she was going round taking it out on everyone she'd ever known. Of course I believed him. I wanted to believe him, and what other explanation could there be?

When I thought about it later I got a cold feeling in the pit of my stomach. What I'd actually seen was a girl who, unlike me, had escaped from Leo. Who knows if the story about the baby was true, and if it was, how had she lost it? I didn't want to know, but in a strange way I envied her, for she'd managed to get away. If only I'd done the same, so much pain could have been avoided, and I would have finished my degree and moved on to the career I'd always dreamed of.

It's true what they say about hindsight, it really is a wonderful thing.

I recalled our day out, not long after Leo and I started seeing each other, when Amy and the rest of my housemates decided we'd go to the beach at the weekend.

The weather had been beautiful for the previous few days, and it was forecast to continue, so we thought we'd make the best of it and dip our toes in the Brighton water.

I asked my housemates if I could invite Leo to come with us and they agreed – although I sensed a certain puzzling reluctance. I couldn't wait to tell him. However, his reaction wasn't what I expected either, he seemed almost annoyed I'd made the arrangements without asking him first. I started to think I didn't understand people at all.

We did go to the beach, but it wasn't the day of fun I'd anticipated. Leo was constantly at my side, influencing every decision: when to swim and when to come out of the water, when to apply sun cream, when to eat or drink. He did his best to keep us apart from the others, as if we were there on our own, and I was embarrassed at the way he cut everyone else out of our conversations and didn't want to join the impromptu game of beach volleyball they set up. However, his attentiveness, compliments and kind words blinded me to his controlling behaviour. The uneasy thought that I wasn't having a good time was brushed aside by the unbelievable fact that this good-looking, clever and loving man only wanted to be with me. Nevertheless I made the decision that in future I would keep trips out with my friends and my time with Leo separate.

Our whirlwind romance led very quickly to marriage, and as I had no family and Leo's family were in Russia, he decided we'd have a quick no-fuss wedding – so that, in his words, they wouldn't feel as though they were missing out. I thought of inviting Sheila and Terry, but Leo said that as it was such a small wedding he didn't think it was fair to expect them to travel all that way. I was disappointed, but convinced myself he was probably right. They weren't getting any younger and Brighton was almost two hundred miles away from their home in Norfolk. So I sent them a letter saying I'd met a wonderful man and was going to get married, and I'd bring him to meet them as soon as I could. At the time I really thought I would, and I was touched by their reply saying they'd love to meet him and asking what we would like for a wedding present.

On the morning of the wedding I awoke with butterflies in my stomach. I was so excited. Even though I knew it wasn't going to be the wedding most girls dream of, I was happy to be marrying the man I loved and looking forward to spending the rest of my life with him. I'd originally intended to wear something special, but Leo told me not to bother, reasoning that it was only going to be a low key affair after all, and we'd have a proper ceremony when we'd graduated and were earning money. This made perfect sense, as I certainly didn't have any spare cash, and Leo paid for the licence and the register office, so I couldn't complain. He was right when he said it would be a low key affair, as the wedding was almost a non-event. It was held at Brighton Town Hall Register Office, the grandeur of which far outshone the occasion, and we were casually dressed with a couple of our friends as witnesses. Although they weren't actually our friends, they were his. I'd suggested asking Amy and a couple of others, but he reasoned you couldn't invite people to a wedding without putting on some kind of reception, and neither of us had the money for that. He said his friends would understand, and they'd disappear after the ceremony, but he didn't want to disappoint my friends or they would think badly of him. He dressed it up by saying he wanted me all to himself, and talked again about doing something special when we both graduated. So I went along with it, even though it didn't feel right.

He then suggested it might be best not to tell my friends until after the event, and everything was arranged quickly and in secret. I can still remember how hurt Amy was when I finally told her. It didn't help that she didn't like Leo to begin with, and I realised that in making the choices I had, I'd totally disregarded her feelings, firmly putting Leo first. My relationship with Amy never fully recovered.

We'd managed to rent a one bedroom flat not far

from campus, and moved out of our student accommodation the same day as our wedding to set up home together. Although a step up from some of the shared student digs off campus, the flat was basic. It was described as furnished, but the furniture was sparse, old and tired. The rooms were small, the kitchen greasy and the windows grimy. In fact the whole flat would have benefitted from a good clean, but at least it was ours, and I immediately got to work with a mop and scrubbing brush. Leo left me to it, saying he had to go and sort out things with the landlord, and before too long the whole flat looked and smelt better. Although it would have been nice to give it a coat of paint, at least I'd thought to get some cleaning materials. Though with limited funds, water and detergent had to do the job. When I finally finished, still with no sign of Leo returning, I was quite proud of the result, even though I couldn't help feeling it was a bizarre way to spend a wedding day.

At first it felt romantic playing 'house' with the man of my dreams, but it became quite a sheltered life without me realising. I went to lectures and came straight home. Leo wasn't keen on mixing with any of my friends and kept reiterating that we were enough for each other. However, there was a definite change in the way my friends behaved around me; I hardly saw anything of Amy, and gone was the old friendly banter. In its place was a reticence, and what I could only describe as a kind of embarrassment. At break times and lunchtimes everyone seemed to form tight groups which didn't include me, and I wondered what I'd done to upset them. My years in care had equipped me to deal with rejection, and I'd seen more than my fair share of spitefulness and isolation, but I thought I'd left that all behind me and that I fitted in well, so I couldn't understand what had gone wrong. I told myself it was their loss, carrying on alone as though everything was fine. I wondered if they were jealous because I'd got the guy, but it still hurt, and I was very lonely.

I didn't think of it at the time, but later I wondered if Leo had said something to them, as it was almost as though they were afraid to mix with me.

I compensated for my lack of friends by putting everything into my marriage, broadening my cooking skills and making us appetising meals on the old gas stove. I took pride in keeping the flat spotless, and really looked forward to the times when we were at home together. Unfortunately it wasn't long before I noticed these times were becoming less frequent, and was disappointed to discover Leo was still seeing his friends, coming home later and later each day. I would rush home after lectures to prepare a meal and be ready for him to arrive, yet he was often late and had clearly been drinking. He was never drunk, but he was a little more demanding, and he began to find fault with things.

Firstly, it was how I looked. When I made an effort and tried to look nice he would ask me if I was seeing someone else, or suggested that I was hoping to attract someone. If I wore casual clothes and no makeup he accused me of being slovenly and not caring what I looked like. He said it was an insult to him if I no longer wanted to make any effort. His remarks always hurt, but he was only belligerent when he'd had a drink, and I constantly wished he'd give the student bar a miss and come straight home.

He was never violent towards me back then, and was always very sorry and loving when he'd sobered up. It was after one of these occasions when he turned up with the puppy. It was a sweet thing, some kind of terrier cross, with lots of character and a great will to please. I called him Terry – Terry the Terrier – because the name also reminded me of my last foster parents, and I loved him straight away. I was really pleased with Leo's gift. It was as though he'd realised I was lonely, and this was therefore evidence of how caring and loving he could be – although neither of us had the first idea of how to look after a pup.

Terry was a bright dog, and we soon formed a bond. I taught him all manner of things and he was quick to learn. I couldn't wait to show Leo the tricks he could perform, and would go through his repertoire when he arrived home from uni. Disappointingly, Leo took little interest. He said I obviously didn't have enough to occupy me, and that perhaps I'd do better to clean and cook rather than play with a puppy. I was hurt, yet also angry, as the comments were unjust. I always made sure the flat was clean and our food was ready, but I kept my feelings under control and stopped showing Leo what Terry could do.

At first, everything was okay. Terry meant I had a reason to go for walks, and I really enjoyed these outings. Whenever I had a free period I would rush home and take him to Stanmer Park. There were many other dogs and dog walkers there, which meant I often had a conversation with someone – a real treat for me. I decided not to tell Leo about these walks as I guessed he wouldn't be pleased.

When, I wonder, did I first understand this need for deceit? I instinctively knew that going for a walk and talking to other dog walkers wouldn't be amongst Leo's 'allowable' activities, and I had started to realise how few things were.

Then, as Terry grew, he started to annoy Leo. Greeting him when he got home was seen as him being over-excited and in need of discipline, so being a wise little dog Terry stopped doing it. Then Leo said the dog ignored him and was not worth keeping. When a couple of pieces of the landlord's furniture got nibbled, Leo was enraged. He told me Terry would have to go, and when I tried to explain that he wasn't a bad puppy, simply a bored one, Leo said he wished he had time to be bored, but he was too busy providing for me so I could sit at home and play with a useless dog.

Not long after this, I came home from lectures to what appeared to be an empty flat. There was no sign of Terry. I searched every room, which didn't take long, and there in the wardrobe I found his poor little body in a dustbin bag, very bloody and very dead. I sobbed and sobbed with his broken body on my lap until I heard Leo arrive home.

'Oh you've found him,' he said. His voice was flat, emotionless, almost dismissive. He said Terry had run out of the flat and been hit by a car, that he'd brought him back inside while he decided what to do with his body. I knew this must be a lie, but I said nothing. Terry couldn't run out of the flat, down the stairs and through a closed front door – and why would he? Then I saw the dark stain on the shoes Leo was wearing. I knew the truth, but I refused to believe it.

'Well you had an unnatural relationship with him anyway, so perhaps it's a good job he got himself killed,' he said.

And that was the end of it. Terry was never mentioned again. I assume Leo must have disposed of the body like useless trash, but I blanked it from my mind.

Chapter 3

I started to attend fewer lectures, as Leo insisted there was no real need for me to graduate. He was going to be a big earner and my future was secure. At first I tried to make him see how much it meant to me – it wasn't just about money, it was about self-esteem – but his answer was that I should have more than enough self-esteem being married to him. I really wanted to graduate and still loved learning, but it wasn't the uni experience any more, and he did everything to discourage me. He told me he thought it more important that I learned to be a good wife rather than the teacher I'd always dreamed of being. He softened the blow with a smile and a loving caress, so I gave in and gave up on my dreams.

I wasn't quite sure which part of "good wife" I was still required to learn. I cooked, I cleaned, I tried hard with my appearance – aiming for neat and tidy without any hint of cheap or tarty – and I really tried to please him in every other way, even though it seemed this was becoming less achievable every day. In the end I did what I always did. I complied. It was something I used to do in unfamiliar foster homes when I thought it best to be invisible. It hadn't been necessary for many years, yet I found the familiar form of retreat very easy to fall back into. That was when I started to lose my own identity,

One thing I did try to speak to Leo about was family planning, and he agreed I musn't get pregnant. However, he blocked every attempt I made to get any kind of help with this, and blatantly refused to take any precautions himself.

Before long I wasn't going to lectures at all any more, and had accepted that my graduation wouldn't be happening. I'd lost contact with my so-called friends; although I seriously doubted if any of them had been real friends, as they'd made no effort to contact me to see if I was okay. I did think of trying to ring Amy, but Leo had recently 'accidentally' dropped my mobile phone in a sink full of water. The promised replacement never materialised. The landline had long since been deemed an unnecessary waste of money, so I had no way of contacting anyone.

Neither could I go anywhere; my Micra had become Leo's Micra. After all, he needed it to get to lectures, and I had no money to pay for the tax and insurance, let alone the petrol. Leaving the flat was discouraged – where on earth did I want to go? I had no money for bus fares and, as Leo said, he could get me anything I needed. The Falmer campus was several miles outside Brighton itself and our flat was close by, making getting into Brighton without transport or money unachievable. All my dreams of walking on the beach and swimming in the sea now seemed a world away. Shopping was ordered online and delivered, but the order checked over before payment to ensure I wasn't wasting Leo's money. Even personal items such as sanitary products didn't escape his scrutiny, or comments about the expense. However, this was all okay, because he told me how much he loved me and how he only wanted to keep me safe. And although his words were often quite brutal, there was still no physical abuse. Not quite yet.

Then I missed my period, and a cold, hard dread began to eat away at me. My knowledge of pregnancy and childbirth was sketchy to say the least – little more than the facts I'd learned in biology at school – but enough to know I was pregnant. Part of me was excited. Here was something I could succeed at; I could be a mother and I was determined I would be a good one. Whatever the reason had been for my own parents giving me away, the same wasn't going to happen to this baby. My baby would be loved and cherished as I should have been. I wasn't sure how Leo would react, although I was fairly certain he wouldn't be pleased. This was definitely not part of his life plan, but perhaps he would surprise me.

I hid it for as long as I could, but when I started throwing up in the mornings I knew I'd have to tell him. I decided to try to make the news a positive thing. I cooked his favourite spaghetti bolognese and put a couple of cans of beer in the fridge to chill. I took what I thought was just the right amount of trouble over my appearance, and then I waited. It was a long wait; he didn't get back until after ten, and I was close to falling asleep. He didn't want anything to eat, so I automatically covered the bolognese, hoping it would keep for the next day. When he saw what I was doing, he announced that he didn't eat leftovers and threw it in the bin, saucepan and all. I was shocked, I'd never seen him like this before. I tried to placate him, asking about his day and making small talk, yet without any warning he suddenly struck me hard across the face. As I reeled back in horror he started to lift his hand to do it again.

'Please, Leo,' I shouted, 'please don't hurt me. I'm sorry.'

His whole face had altered, and for the first time I was afraid. In an effort to stop the onslaught I told him about the baby.

'Leo, don't, please don't... I'm pregnant!'

In my innocence I really thought this would bring him to his senses, and I held my breath as the words sunk in. Yet the only change my announcement brought about was a greater intensity to his anger. It was the first beating I endured, and it set the pattern for what was to come. That very first time, the shock was almost as bad as the considerable pain. I couldn't believe what was happening to me, and I didn't recognise the man who was doing it. I tried to defend myself, but this had little effect on Leo's furious onslaught, and I realised with horror that most of his punches were deliberately aimed at my stomach. I tried to bend over to protect myself, but he pushed my head further down and brought his knee up to connect with my chin. That was when I crumpled to the floor.

It all stopped as suddenly as it had started, and when it was over he calmly told me to clean myself up and get to bed. In my shame and humiliation, and no doubt suffering from shock, that's exactly what I did, only to be joined by him a few minutes later as if nothing had happened. That was also the first time he took me in anger. It was almost an extension of the beating, with little or no involvement from me other than my mute compliance. As he took what he wanted, he repeated I had to learn obedience, and that he would make sure I did.

When he'd finished, he turned over and went straight to sleep. I knew he was asleep because of his snoring, now a regular thing after a drinking session. However, there was no sleep for me; I lay cold and trembling, feeling as though I'd been in some kind of accident. My face was sore, yet more worrying was the pain in my stomach. I'd only just come to terms with being pregnant and now I was sure I was going to lose the baby. I pressed my hands across my middle to try to feel any movement. However, it was still early days, and in truth I hadn't felt any movement even before the attack. I checked between my legs to see if I was losing blood, but could only feel the evidence of Leo's assault – for that is what it was. He had raped me.

At some point I must have dozed off in spite of my pain, and when I woke up again it was daylight. I knew straight away that things were no better, and I eased myself out of bed, wincing with every movement. When Leo got up he behaved as if nothing had happened. He ate the breakfast I'd prepared for him and then left for uni, but there was a parting shot.

'I'll see what I can get sorted out for the abortion,

although it will cost money we can barely afford. It'll have to be done on the quiet as we don't want people knowing. You keep out of sight today – you look a mess.'

And with that he left.

Keep out of sight? Who on earth was I likely to see? I couldn't believe he was planning to arrange an abortion without discussion or any thought of what I wanted. But that was the new pattern of my life. My opinions were neither sought nor heard. Any attempt to express my own thoughts or to exert a will of my own was met with punishment, and I honestly believe he thought he could save the cost of the abortion by doing the job himself.

I didn't see anyone, as I was kept in the flat as a virtual prisoner. I had no money, no transport and no phone, and as I didn't even have my little dog anymore I had no reason to step outside. I did think of making a run for it, but where could I run to? Where could I be sure he wouldn't find me? He started hinting that he believed I suffered from mental health issues, and I realised he probably told other people the same, so even if I did manage to escape he would simply tell anyone who helped me that I was ill and force me to go back.

The abortion didn't happen, as – much to Leo's annoyance – by the time he'd found someone willing to do it on the quiet, I was too far gone. He would still have gone ahead, but even a back street abortionist has standards, refusing to do it when they could plainly see how far along I was. Once again this was my fault, and I was punished accordingly, then virtually ignored for the rest of the pregnancy.

Ignored, that is, until the day of Leo's graduation, when I dared to ask if I could go to the ceremony.

'How can you go anywhere looking like that? You look hideous and none of your clothes fit you anymore. What were you thinking of wearing? Jeans with the waist left open, or perhaps you could get into some tracksuit bottoms? You disgust me.'

So I stayed at home while he collected his degree. He came home late and drunk, and that was the beating that brought on the birth. He was way too early, but that's when my baby came into this world. It's funny, I still don't think of him as anything other than "the baby", because Leo – in a rare moment of interest – insisted on naming him the English version of his own name. He was given the name Leonard, or Leo for short, but I knew I could never bring myself to call this darling boy the same name as my husband.

***

So, six months after my baby's birth, on an ordinary morning, no different to any other, after a beating which had been no better, no worse than a hundred more before it, there I was, finally planning to leave and take the baby with me. I had no real idea how I'd do it, but I reminded myself that when I was younger I'd had no idea how I'd get to university either. All I knew was that I must save myself and my baby; no one else was going to do it for us.

I started to form a plan, and the first thing I did was write another letter to my foster parents. I had no access to any other type of communication and wasn't even sure how I'd post it, but thought if it turned up at their house without a stamp on, they would surely pay the excess. As it turned out, I didn't need to do that, for in the wallet section of my almost unused purse I found a book of second class stamps left over from the last Christmas of my freedom.

I carefully composed a letter telling Sheila and Terry all that had happened to me, including the beatings, and even about the death of the dog, yet stressing they mustn't do anything about it. I knew this was a tall order, and I was very worried they would report it to the police or come flying to my rescue, both of which could end in disaster. All I wanted them to do was to give me a temporary home as they had done before – this time with my baby. Deep down I hoped they might be able to look after him while I found work to support us; but one thing at a time. I was ashamed to ask for charity, but I owned nothing, and when I left I could take nothing. So I wrote the letter, stuck on the stamp, and carefully chose a time when I knew it was safe to pop out to the post box at the end of the road. I was so concerned about leaving the baby on his own that I ran down the road clutching my letter like some kind of mad woman.

That was the first part of my plan in place. I hadn't dared to ask my foster parents to respond, and I didn't put an address at the top of the letter, knowing all post was scrutinised. I would have to set off in the hope they'd received it and would make us welcome. As well as the stamps, I was surprised and delighted to find a £20 note and some change in my purse. It had been there since the day I got married; not enough to get us all the way to Norfolk, but enough to get us away from Brighton. Then I'd have to think again. My old bank card was also in my purse, but I could see it had expired. Did I even have a bank account any longer? Who knew what Leo had done while I'd been shut away from the world?

I continued to plan. What would I need for the baby? Would I be able to carry him, as I had no pram or pushchair? I practised making a sling of sorts from a pashmina I still had from the good old days, but I wasn't sure it was strong enough to hold him. I needed my hands free to carry his bag of things, and now I was no longer breastfeeding, that was quite a lot of stuff. I had enjoyed breastfeeding once I got the hang of it, and I knew it was the best thing for my boy, but for some reason it enraged Leo and I had to try to do it when he wasn't around. Then, after a particularly bad beating, my milk simply dried up.

When I first brought the baby home the health visitor tried to visit a couple of times. Leo managed to fob them off by telling them that both the baby and I were asleep.

When they left, saying they'd come back another time, Leo ranted about interfering busybodies and told me not to let anyone in. They did try a few more times, but after finding me repeatedly "out" they eventually stopped bothering.

Then my milk dried up and I was terrified the baby would starve. I knew I'd have to ask Leo to buy some powdered formula. He grudgingly agreed, but complained about the price of it, and told me I was a failure as a mother if I couldn't provide milk for my baby. He found it was cheaper to buy in packs of six, and so he only bought the first batch and then told me to add them to my online shopping. This meant we always had plenty in the cupboard and I knew there'd be enough to take with me.

I would need to make up enough feed to last for the journey, however long that might take, and make sure I had enough nappies as well. He didn't have many clothes, but he'd need a couple of sleep suits, and I needed to make sure everything I took would last for a while as my foster parents were unlikely to have any baby stuff.

I planned to present myself and my baby to the local authorities as homeless and destitute, and hopefully I'd be eligible for some kind of financial help, and perhaps even accommodation, until I could find a job to support us. The more I planned, the more optimistic I became. I discussed it all in full with the baby, telling him it would be better, that he would have clothes and toys and somewhere to play safely. When he stared up at me with an incredibly knowing look on his little face, I actually started to believe it would really happen.

Somehow these secret plans got me through the next couple of weeks while I endured further beatings and verbal abuse. Deep inside I held on to the thought that it would all be over soon. Little did I know how prophetic that was.

Chapter 4

I chose a Friday to leave, working on the theory that Leo was always late home on a Friday. That was my first mistake.

I spent the day getting things together, at the same time keeping them hidden in case Leo came home unexpectedly. I was fairly sure that if I fed and changed the baby at around 4 p.m., then we could leave by five and have at least a good three or four hours start. I couldn't go any earlier, as Leo sometimes came home at lunchtime, and when he left it was usually the baby's feed time again. So I waited it out. I reasoned that once I fed him he would be sleepy and easier to travel with, and as it was a Friday, Leo may well stop off at the student bar before coming home, in which case he may not arrive back until nine or ten. We would be long gone by then and not so easy to follow.

I didn't pack anything for myself; I would simply have to manage, as there was only so much I could stuff in a rucksack. I found an old timetable for the buses which came past the flat regularly and stopped at the end of the road. Although I didn't know where they went, chances were they would end up at the bus station where the National Express coaches ran from. I crossed my fingers that the information was still up to date, as I had no idea how long it had been in the flat. Hopefully there was one at 5.10 p.m. and this would work fine if I didn't hang about.

It was perhaps a rather random plan, but I believed it was our only chance, and I knew that once I'd gone Leo wouldn't have any idea of where to search. He'd kept me a virtual prisoner for so long that he knew I wasn't in touch with anyone and – except for the letter to Terry and Sheila – I'd been careful not to involve other people. He wouldn't be able to learn anything from my friends – not that I had friends any longer – and with no idea of my foster parents' surname or address he couldn't look for me there.

I was almost ready to leave, but I wanted to take the last box of powdered milk with me, and my rucksack was at bursting point. I'd waited until the last minute because I wasn't sure whether I'd need to open it before I left, but in the end I'd managed to make up the bottles and his last feed without it. I'd put the other three boxes in the bottom of the bag, but I realised this last one wouldn't squash down enough to fit in. I didn't want to leave it as I had no idea when I'd be able to buy more, so I decided to take out the inside packet and dump the box. I started to pull at the sealed top, but I needed scissors. I rummaged in the drawer, yet couldn't see them, and conscious of the time I decided to take everything out. I piled the cutlery on the worktop, working fast now, and at the very bottom I found the scissors. I cut the top off the box, took the packet out, and pushed it into the top of the rucksack, throwing the cutlery and the scissors back into the drawer.

Right, time to go. With my heart hammering in my chest, I went to fetch the baby.

He was still sleepy and didn't murmur when I picked him up. Grabbing the rucksack in my other hand I made for the door. It was almost 5 p.m. now, and I was beginning to panic. I couldn't afford to miss the bus and risk being found standing out in the street when Leo arrived home. But when I opened the door, he was standing there.

I instinctively squeezed the baby tight, waking him up. Startled, he started to cry, and without any warning Leo hit me so hard in the face that he knocked me backwards. As I fell, he grabbed the baby from the homemade sling, but not, as I quickly realised, to save him. I was up on my feet in an instant.

'So you thought you could leave me did you? And

take this bloody little nuisance with you. Well I'm telling you now, you'll never leave, but this one can go!'

He took hold of the screaming baby by one leg and threw him as hard as he could across the room, where he hit the wall and fell to the floor in a silent heap. In the second before he turned to me, I spotted the large carving knife I'd accidentally left out on the worktop. I stepped swiftly across the room, scarcely aware of my own movements, gripped the smooth wooden handle in both hands and held it tight.

I didn't intend to kill him, I simply wanted to get away, to pick up my baby and run. But he was coming at me, like he always did, and I knew he would hurt both me and my baby again if I didn't take action. I was rooted to the spot with terror, but I held the big knife out in both hands in front of me, and as he reached out towards me it went into him. Did I push it? Had I stabbed him? I didn't know, but he fell to the floor in front of me and the knife was sticking out of his chest. I dropped down beside him, thinking that if I could pull the blade out it would be like it hadn't happened. Then I thought again, and realised that while he wasn't moving I could still get away – but first I must get to my baby. I staggered to my feet and ran across to where he'd landed.

It was too late.

His crumpled body looked much the same as when I'd held him, but his poor little head was smashed. I dropped to my knees beside him, but there was no sound or movement. He was dead, and so was his father.

I stood up and ran to the bathroom, where I was sick over and over again until I had nothing left inside me. I was an empty shell, my head pounding as I shook uncontrollably, sweat pouring off me.

My little baby boy was dead, and it was my fault. I should have protected him, but I'd failed, and he'd lost his precious life. I was useless, it was all my fault. All my fault. I sank back down to the floor. I couldn't call for help as I had no phone, I couldn't go out and leave my darling baby boy. It was my fault, all my fault. I wished I was dead too.

I don't know how many hours I sat there on the bathroom floor. It got dark and it got cold and still I sat. What could I do? Where could I go? All the old familiar questions, but now it was just me, and I wasn't worth saving.

I saw the blue lights shining through the window before they came into the flat. Where did they come from? Who called them? A muddle of green and blue uniforms. Voices, one a woman's, a woman in a green uniform who came up and put her arms around me. I couldn't move and I couldn't speak. She helped me up, wrapped a blanket around me and led me outside. I heard someone mention forensics, but she replied that she must first find out if I was hurt. She led me to a brightly lit, warm ambulance and told me to lie down. She sat beside me and held my hand before checking me over for injuries. I knew one side of my face must be swollen as I could feel how tight it was, but what I couldn't see was the gash on my cheek from where Leo's ring had caught me, and the purple bruising around my eye. Neither had I noticed I was covered in blood; my hands were soaked and my face and hair were splattered. The knees of my jeans had soaked up my poor little baby's blood when I knelt down to check if he was still alive, and the onslaught on Leo had covered me with his. Thinking back, the young paramedic must have been horrified, but she gave no sign and was kind and gentle with me.

They took me to the hospital, where they cleaned and patched me up. I was uncommunicative and they couldn't find out from me what had happened. Then two uniformed police officers came into the cubicle and I was formally arrested on suspicion of the murder of both my husband and my son. I listened as the officer read me my rights and asked if I had anything to say. What could I say? I was a murderer, and although I knew I hadn't killed the baby, I might as well have done, because I'd failed to protect him. So, yes, I was a murderer, and I deserved whatever was coming to me.

The days which followed were cold and dark. They didn't put me in a cell, as I was classed as vulnerable, but the place they took me to was far more frightening than any cell. I was placed under supervised care in a mental hospital, where the background noise was a combination of random shouting, clanging trolleys, moaning and classical music.

I don't know whether I was simply sedated or prescribed other anti-depressant drugs, but I lost a couple of months of my life to dark dreams, where Leo chased me with a carving knife and my baby talked to me and begged for help. When awake, I had no awareness or recollection of the things I had done, but for the most part I was asleep in a land of terror and recriminations. I didn't communicate, as I had nothing to say. I was compliant and caused them no trouble, yet when I screamed out in my sleep they came and stuck needles in me which put me back into the nightmare I was trying to escape. When I was conscious I had no interest in my future or what would become of me. I didn't think of Leo at all, and when the pictures of my beautiful baby boy came into my head they were replaced with the last view I had of his poor dead body; best not to think at all, best just to sleep.

I have no idea how long I was in there or when I started talking again, but as soon as I was able to be interviewed they came: policeman, lawyers, social workers. They were all the same to me and I had nothing to say to them. For what felt like weeks, a succession of these people came to my room. They all tried different tactics to engage with me, yet somehow I couldn't fathom out what they were saying, what their words meant, and I decided to keep quiet and pretend they weren't there.

Then I had a visit from a smart young woman who told me she was my legal representative. I didn't know why I would need one, as Leo was dead and no threat any more. But gradually I remembered. I was being charged with murder; not just the murder of Leo, but of my baby as well. I started to cry, long racking sobs which came from somewhere deep inside me. I couldn't speak, I couldn't think. I simply wept. The lawyer looked out of her depth as I continued to heave and sob.

'I'll come back when you're feeling better, and then perhaps we can have a chat.' With that, she backed out of my room and left.

Eventually, when I was too exhausted to cry anymore, I fell asleep. When I woke up I was ready to tell my story.

Chapter 5

The lawyer's name was Caroline Blackwell, and the next time she visited me both of us were in a better frame of mind. I think my medication must have been reduced, as I felt awake and alert for the first time in months, and was now filled with a grim determination to tell people how my lovely baby boy had died, and what an evil monster his father had been.

I hadn't taken any notice of this woman when she'd visited me before. But today was different; I was ready to talk. I took a good look at Caroline, as though I would be able to discern exactly who she was by her appearance. She wore a smart, almost masculine, pinstripe trouser suit, but this was feminised by the soft pink open-necked blouse which revealed an elegant neck. Although her dark hair had been cut into a neat and professional bob, it was the type of hair that had a slight natural curl which defied control, and the sleek outline was already showing rebellious hairs that curled the opposite way. Her eyes were surprisingly blue, which was slightly unnerving with such dark hair, especially as they were framed by dark lashes, but they were wide and friendly with a sparkle that promised humour.

I could see she was very young, not much older than me, and yet I felt years older. Her fresh face had not seen the horrors I had endured, and I feared she would struggle to believe or understand the story I was about to tell. However, her smile was open and genuine, so I decided there and then that here was someone I could trust.

Once I started talking it seemed I couldn't stop. I told Caroline everything right from the beginning – about my various foster homes, especially the final one with Terry and Sheila, the couple who'd helped me so much. I explained how excited I'd been about going to university, and how I'd met and fallen in love with Leo almost instantly, believing myself lucky to have won the heart of this wonderful man. I told her about my hopes and dreams of becoming a teacher, and how hard I worked in my first year before I met him. I told her I didn't see what was happening at first and only realised I had no friends left after they'd disappeared, that I had no idea what Leo told them or why they didn't try to find me, but by the time I dropped out of uni no one seemed to want to find out the truth. I explained I could now see the futility of trying to leave him – my plan would never have worked – but I truly didn't believe he would kill his own baby.

Then I told her about my life with Leo before that fateful day: the beatings, the threats, my fear for my baby. I explained that although I didn't think Leo intended to hurt him when he was rational, I was aware of the terrible danger the baby was in when he set out to punish me, because then he was no longer rational. I told her about the death of my beloved puppy and how I had feared for my own life more than once.

Then I told her about the day, the awful day, when my poor innocent baby lost his life and I lost my mind. I told her about my plan to leave and how carefully I'd thought it through. It was somehow important to explain to her that I'd talked it over with the baby; although I realised how silly I must have sounded. I suppose it was a pathetic attempt to justify what I did by believing that we had somehow agreed on the plan. I took time out of my tale to tell her how he'd smiled and gurgled when I told him what we would do, that he'd even wrapped his little fist around my finger. I knew I was prevaricating, though to her credit Caroline didn't try to hurry me, as if realising I needed a moment to dwell in this joyous memory before I entered the dark world of what came next.

I told the story just as it had happened. It was now

all so clear in my mind: my search for the scissors which led to the carving knife being left out on the worktop, the sardonic smile on Leo's face when I opened the door to see him standing there. The feeling of having the baby wrenched from my arms and then the horrific realisation that he was holding him by one ankle and throwing him across the room. I had to stop then, I couldn't go on, and I rushed to the toilet to be sick.

When I returned, Caroline looked as sick as I felt, and she had tears in her eyes. I hadn't been sure whether she would believe me, but I had little doubt now that she knew I was telling the truth. The next part of my story was blurred in my mind; the clarity of my baby's death was overshadowed by the cloudy memory of what followed. I tried to remember how it happened, closing my eyes to attempt to bring it back to the front of my mind. All I could see was the shocked look on Leo's face as he felt the knife go in and fell to the floor.

Up to this point, Caroline had said very little, and other than asking me if I was all right or needed a break, she'd simply let me talk. Now it was as though she could tell I needed encouragement to face this part of my story, and she came over and touched my hand.

'Take your time, Lydia. There's no rush, but try to remember how Leo ended up with the knife in him. Where was he? Where were you? Where was the knife?'

It was as though she was speaking from a great distance; I could hear the words but somehow couldn't process them in my mind. Leo, knife, dead – yes, that all made sense – but not how, why, or even who. My mind had sanitised this memory by almost obliterating it, but with Caroline's encouragement I tried very hard to remember.

I'd gone straight across to pick up the knife when I noticed it lying on the worktop. I'd never looked for a weapon or anything to defend myself with when Leo had beaten me before, but this was about defending my baby. Even then I don't think I intended to use it. It was only to keep Leo away from me, to stop him hurting me before I could get to my baby. I could remember holding the knife out in front of my waist, but still Leo kept smiling and still he kept coming towards me. I remembered waving it at him, shouting at him to get back, but he laughed out loud and held his hands up in mock surrender as though he knew I wouldn't use it. Then he stopped laughing and spoke. It was when I remembered Leo's words that I had the flashback. I knew without doubt he hadn't walked into the knife. I stabbed him. I could remember the knife going into his chest and the force I used to push it home. And I remembered why. It was when he told me, in a terrifyingly cold voice, that he was going to take the knife from me, that he would cut me into ribbons and make sure no other man would want me, then he would slice up my baby and get rid of it. Yes, that was why; I stabbed him with all my might, and drove the knife into him, all the way to the handle.

When I finished, there were no questions. Caroline sat in stunned silence, and I felt as though I'd run a marathon. I was totally exhausted, tears streaming down my face. All I wanted was to go to sleep, but I was racked with sobs and struggling to breathe. Caroline dropped her professional persona for a moment, came across to my chair and hugged me. It was brief yet sincere, and it gave me the few minutes I needed to regain some kind of composure.

When she thought I was ready to go on, Caroline told me she had recorded everything I'd said, but would delete it all if I wasn't happy. She explained she'd recorded it for her own use, to ensure she didn't forget any details, but would delete it in front of me if I wasn't comfortable with it.

Did I care? Was I uncomfortable? I suddenly had no feelings at all; I was dead inside, cried-out and exhausted, and when Caroline stood up to leave she took the recording with her.

It was a couple of days later when she came back to see me, and told me she'd been in touch with my foster parents, who had shown her my letter. She said that with this letter, if I was prepared to let other people hear the recording of our last interview, she thought she would be able to prove my case as self-defence, and there would then be no murder conviction. I didn't care who listened to the recording, nor about whether I was found guilty. I was guilty. I killed Leo, and I wasn't sorry. I could see that after all the beatings and the way he came towards me that day, I did act in self-defence, but my poor baby was dead and that was my fault. So I was still guilty. I started to wonder about what had happened to my wee boy? Had he been buried or cremated? Was there a little grave somewhere with his name on it?

'So what do you think, Lydia? Are you happy for me to share the recording?'

I nodded.

***

I don't think I was sedated after that day, and I gradually returned to the hospital routine, but with more clarity than before. I knew I didn't want to stay in this place, but could think of no alternative. There was nowhere I wanted to go and no one I wanted to see, and I was beginning to settle into the safety of my current situation and accept there was nothing more. At least here, nothing was expected of me. I didn't have to please anyone and, as long as I didn't offend, they more or less left me alone. I had no responsibility, no decisions to make; I didn't even have to worry about what to wear, as all of this was taken care of. As a punishment it wasn't too bad, and I certainly didn't deserve anything better.

Time went by – days, weeks, maybe months, I had no idea. Each day was the same: the noises, the food, the view from the window. Nothing changed. And then Caroline arrived again.

'All charges have been dropped, Lydia. You have been found not guilty by reason of self-defence, and you are now free to leave here, get on with your life and forget all about Leo.'

She said this in such an upbeat way, and although I knew she thought this was wonderful news, it felt like anything but. Get on with my life? Forget about Leo? Did she really believe this was possible? Were we not going to mention the little life which was lost, or the permanent ache inside me? The raw yearning to hold him close, to protect and shield him as I'd failed to do on that awful day. I made it happen; it had been my stupid idea to get away for my own selfish reasons. That was what brought my baby to his end; I was not fit to have been his mother.

The following day I found myself 'free', but to do what I wasn't sure. A social worker came to collect me from the hospital and told me Terry and Sheila had agreed I could go and stay with them for as long as I needed. If I decided that wasn't what I wanted to do, then I needn't worry, I wouldn't have to go back to the flat whatever happened. They'd found me a studio flat to use while I made up my mind, and if I decided to stay in Brighton, they would try to find me a more permanent place. There were flats available quite close to the university campus, so perhaps I could re-enrol and finish my degree if that's what I wanted? I knew she was being kind and I resisted the urge to scream at her and tell her to leave me alone. I didn't want to re-enrol at university and I didn't want to stay in Brighton, yet I knew I couldn't go back to Norfolk either. There was nowhere I wanted to be.

As we left the hospital, I had my first real look at what had been home for so many weeks – or was it months? When I arrived it was dark and I'd been sitting in the back of a police car with no interest in where I was going. In daylight I could see the beauty of the house, which offered no clues as to its purpose. It looked like a rectory or grand country house.

Built from red brick, the upper storey was softened by cream rendering. There were uniform lines of Georgian windows, and rounded bow windows top and bottom, which gave a warm and welcoming appearance to the whole house. There was nothing here to suggest a secure institution, and the vast grounds resembled the parkland usually found surrounding grand country manors. As the social worker, whose name I couldn't remember, drove me out of these grounds, I looked back and wanted to scream at her to stop. I was being taken away from safety, from a place I'd become used to – or perhaps resigned to – but nevertheless a place where I didn't have to think. I wanted to go back, not face this terrifying life I was being returned to.

***

The flat was in Bedford Square, one of the once beautiful four storey houses set in square formation close to the seafront. From its obvious grand beginnings, it had gone the way of so many others in this university city and been turned into multiple flats. From the outside, the stuccoed façade, white windows and black wrought iron railings still looked like a Regency townhouse belonging to upper class gentry, and the beautiful gardens which ran down the middle of the square gave an air of space and grandeur which belied its current use. However, as I was shown through the gate at pavement level, and down the steps to the basement flat, I couldn't help feeling I was descending into darkness.

I knew this area from my trips to Brighton in my first year. It was just off the seafront, only a short walk to the town centre, and I realised I was lucky – it could have been a lot worse. It was strange to be given my own key again, handed to me by the social worker as she left, and I was relieved to have my own front door too, as it meant I wouldn't have to mix with anyone in communal hallways.

The flat was bright and clean. It consisted of one main room, with a bed – which also served as a settee – against the right hand wall. Next to it was a chest of drawers, and there was a table and two chairs at the other end of the room. There were two doors on the wall opposite the entrance; the one on the right led to a tiny kitchen with a fridge, hob, microwave and washing machine, and the other to an equally small bathroom. Between the two doors was a bookcase, and on the wall above the table was a TV. The only window was next to the entrance and looked out to the area at the bottom of the steps. In addition, there were some glassed-in grilles at ceiling height, which were at pavement level on the outside and also let in some daylight.

The tiny kitchen was equipped with all the basics: crockery, cutlery and utensils, and even a selection of clean tea towels. When I opened the fridge I saw that they had provided me with milk, butter, bacon, eggs and ham, and had even put a bottle of wine in the door to chill. On further investigation I found a selection of dry goods and everyday groceries in one of the wall cupboards, and some potatoes, onions and a cauliflower in the vegetable rack. Even more surprising were the clothes: a couple of pairs of jeans and a selection of underwear, socks, jumpers and T-shirts in the chest of drawers, all new and in the right size.

The bathroom provided both a bath and an over-bath shower, and there was soap, shampoo, shower gel and towels. Someone had obviously tried hard to ensure I would be clean, tidy and wouldn't go hungry and, although I didn't care what I looked like and couldn't face eating anything, I was touched by their kindness. In the living area, as well as the television on the wall, there were books on the bookshelf and some flowers on the table. All in all it was a clean and pleasant space, and someone had done their best to make it homely for me.

Almost automatically I walked into the kitchen and put the kettle on, then went back to the bookshelf and flicked through the books. There were novels and cookery books jumbled together; they seemed to have been arranged by size rather than subject matter. I suspected they'd probably come from a car boot sale, as there was no rhyme or reason to the selection. As I waited for the kettle to boil, I pulled out a book at random. I saw from the cover it was clearly a holiday read, depicting a beautiful girl in a floaty dress on golden sands, perhaps chosen to take my mind off my situation. Instead, I saw the scene as dark and threatening, the girl only inches away from running into the sea and drowning. I replaced it and pulled out a cookery book. The first page was full of recipes and tips for preparing the perfect Christmas fare for a family – I put that back on the shelf too.

The kettle boiled and I made a cup of tea. I could scarcely remember how to do it, but I managed a weak brew and took it over to the sofa bed. Perhaps there would be something to watch on TV. However, when I turned it on there was no picture, only static and hissing. I couldn't be bothered to fiddle with it, so I switched it off again. I knew there was food in the fridge but I didn't feel like eating either. I realised I was very tired and decided to lie down and try to sleep.

It was dark when I woke up and looked around the unfamiliar space. There I was, alone in the silence of the room, free and yet a prisoner of my own guilt and despair: nothing to look forward to, nothing to plan, no one to miss me, nothing to live for.

I sat up and contemplated putting the light on, but there wasn't anything I wanted to see. I could go out, there was nothing to stop me, but where would I go? Then suddenly I knew; in my mind's eye I saw the cover of the holiday novel again. I only had to walk to the end of the street, cross the road and I would be there.

I pulled the door shut behind me, climbed the steps and turned towards the seafront. I could smell the sea, and as I drew closer the familiar blue railings and steps came into view.

Chapter 6

Time stood still. There was no before, and there would be no after; there was nowhere else to be, only here and now. Looking out to sea, as I had done so often in happier times, I felt both resignation and peace. This dark night was in complete contrast to the bright sunny day when I first brought my hopes and dreams to this university city. Life was full of fun back then, now it was dark and threatening, strengthening my grim determination to do what I must do. But as the waves crashed onto the pebbles, dragging shells, seaweed and lolly sticks back into its foamy mouth, everything which had led me to this point became a blur, and a cold numbness took over my mind and body. I was overwhelmingly tired, tempted to simply lie down on the stony beach and let the waves carry me away. But rational thought told me this wouldn't work; I must drive myself to walk forward and just keep on walking.

The moon was bright, and although I was still some distance from the water's edge, I could see far out across the silver-tipped waves, the lights of small boats bobbing up and down in the distance. There would be people on board, fishing or cruising, probably sleeping at this time of night, carrying on with their ordinary lives, unaware that only a short distance away mine was coming to an end. In other circumstances the scene would have been breathtaking, with the moon sparkling on the water, and I had to concede that my last view of this earth did contain a certain beauty.

Then, unbidden, the pictures came into my mind of another time I'd been on this beach. It was all so long ago and so much had happened since, but I could still remember the feeling of carefree happiness and the sheer joy of life. It had been hot all day, and when lectures were over I'd decided to go to the beach with Amy and Emily. It was a spontaneous decision, and no sooner had we made it than we were on our way to catch the bus. There was still enough of the day left to get some swimming in, enough sun to top up our tans, and we knew most of the crowd would have gone home by then.

The overriding memory of that day was laughter. For some reason we found everything funny. It all started with the people we could see out of the bus window. We'd opted to sit upstairs, right at the front, and had a panoramic view of the pavement below, where people were going about their everyday lives. We decided one of the men we saw looked like a serial killer, but then as we passed him we realised that he was in fact one of our lecturers. We all found this hilarious; that was the kind of daft mood we were in. Then we moved on, teasing each other about our relationships, Emily and I joking with Amy about her boyfriend dilemma. She insisted there was no boyfriend and no dilemma. I pointed out that she was right about there being no boyfriend, but there were several potential candidates, and there was the dilemma. By the time we got to the beach we were aching with laughter and ready for a swim. Everything was perfect.

A shiver passed through me, bringing me back to cold reality and the knowledge that the time for my last walk was here. I wasn't frightened, as that would suggest unwillingness rather than the acceptance I actually felt. Now the time had come, I couldn't stop my mind rewinding back to the horrific scene; the deaths that were mine to atone for. I just wanted it all to be over.

I removed my shoes, jeans and big heavy jumper and put them in a neat pile behind me on the stones. Shivering uncontrollably in my underwear, I took a step forward, and at the same time became aware of the absurdity of getting undressed, as any loss of buoyancy would in fact have aided my purpose. However, the thought of disappearing without a trace left behind was more than I could bear. The neat pile of clothing would at least prove I had existed, even though there was no one left to care.

Once the first step was taken, the way became easier; the biting cold from the coastal wind didn't encourage hesitation, but drove me steadfastly towards the edge of the water. As the first icy trickle touched my foot it took my breath away and I fought the instinct to step back. My heart was hammering in my chest and my breath was coming in short, shallow pants as I forced the other foot to take another step. Yet before I could do so, my eye was caught by the moon glinting on something white, far out to sea. As I strained to see what it was, I heard a faint whining that ended in a despairing wail.

The noise appeared to be coming from the object, and as it came closer I could just make out it was a dog, struggling to reach the water's edge, but being constantly carried back out by the receding tide. No longer aware of the cold, I watched as this brave little dog, desperately keeping its head above the water, frantically paddled, only to be dragged back out, each time turning its head to the shore again in a struggle to survive. Rooted to the spot I watched this drama unfold, touched by the irony of the dog's determination to hang on to life, while I could find nothing to live for. It seemed tragic that this little creature should lose a life it obviously valued highly, when I had no use for mine.

I was now oblivious to the cold and my own situation, and I knew I had to save this dog. Whatever became of me was secondary to this poor animal's desperate plight, and when it disappeared beneath a large wave I realised time was running out. I plunged into the water and struck out towards the spot where I'd last seen the dog. I'd always been a strong swimmer, and within a few seconds I could see it again, coughing and spluttering, yet still paddling for all it was worth back towards the beach. As I got closer it saw me, and as if realising I could help it, the dog changed direction and paddled across

45

to me. As it drew near I grabbed it by the scruff and tried to hold on, but in the confusion only succeeded in pushing it under. It surfaced again, with no apparent animosity, and I had another go. This time I put my arm around its middle and swum one-armed back towards the shore.

As I pulled us up on the beach we were both pretty worn out, and for a moment or two we both lay motionless, gathering our wits and our breath. The dog was the first to move, shaking herself vigorously and licking my face as if encouraging me to do the same. I struggled to my feet and walked back to where I'd left my clothes. Grabbing the thick jumper, I rubbed the little dog down. I realised she was only a youngster, possibly no more than a year old, with no identification and apparently nowhere to go, as she seemed quite happy to stay with me. Yet I knew that couldn't happen. I'd given her the chance to survive she so desperately wanted, but nothing had changed for me; my purpose remained the same.

With a quick pat I said goodbye to the little dog and made my way back to the sea. After my swim it looked almost welcoming; the water wouldn't be so cold now. My tiredness would help, as I would be less inclined to resort to swimming, and if I could get far enough out it would all be over quite soon. As I walked towards the waves I felt something brush my leg. I looked down to see the dog walking along by my side. I tried to shoo her away but she ignored my efforts and walked resolutely forward to the water's edge. I couldn't believe that this little dog was prepared to follow me back into the water which had so nearly claimed her life, and from which she'd been so desperate to escape. However, as I took another step forward into the shallow water, I heard her splashing along beside me. I was overwhelmed, and from somewhere deep inside me all the emotion I had determinedly smothered came bursting forward. I began to cry. Bending to scoop up the dog, I knew I wouldn't walk forward again, for here in my arms was something to live for – a living being which needed me. This tiny dog had saved me, just as much as I'd saved her. Even if it was only short term, she had arrived like a guardian angel, and for now that was enough. As I walked back towards my clothes I put the dog down on the ground.

'Come on Angel, let's go home.'

***

Now I had made the decision to live I was filled with a new sense of purpose. Although I was soaked through I put my clothes back on and pushed my wet feet into my shoes. My jumper was still wet from where I'd rubbed the little dog dry, but I put it on anyway and looked down at my new friend.

'I don't have a lead, Angel, and anyway you don't have a collar, so if you don't want to come with me you don't have to. I'm not much of an owner, but I'll do my best.'

I turned away from the sea and crunched back up the stony beach with my wet feet in my damp shoes. I headed for the steps I'd come down, and it was comforting to know the dog was walking soundlessly along beside me. She was far too light to disturb the pebbles, and my heart went out to this brave little creature, who such a short while ago changed my life, or rather ensured I still had one. I didn't even know if I was allowed to have a dog in my flat, though neither did I care. I had no idea of the time, but guessed it must be the early hours of the morning, so hopefully no one would see me take her in. The building was in darkness, and as all the occupants were likely to be asleep I would need to be quiet. I bent down to scoop Angel up, then held her close, hoping she'd understand the need for silence, feeling her tail thump the side of my body as she tried to lick my face. Opening the metal gate as quietly as I could, I went down the steps to my front door on tiptoe. Then I began to panic. What had I done with my key? Was I locked out? I had no memory of locking the door and reasoned that perhaps I hadn't. Sure enough, when I tried the handle it swung open. I switched on the light and felt round the back of the door, discovering the key exactly where I had left it, still in the lock on the inside. I hadn't intended coming back.

Once inside, I put Angel down, and she rushed around sniffing everything in sight and wagging her tail. I realised I was hungry, so very hungry, and guessed she must be too. I settled on a ham omelette for me, and thought she might enjoy the same, so made two. I put some bread in the toaster, made a coffee, and set down a bowl of warm milk for the dog. We ate like kings, both thoroughly enjoying it. I looked at her as she licked the plate clean and then turned her smiley face towards me. For some reason, I started to laugh. I laughed until tears ran down my cheeks. In the end I wasn't sure if I was laughing or crying, but the release of emotion was so good I didn't care. Angel came and sat beside me as if she too were enjoying the joke, and then she effortlessly jumped up and landed on my lap. I stopped laughing and hugged her tight.

With my stomach full, and my emotion spent, I wanted nothing more than to sleep, so I left all the dishes where they were and without bothering to take off my wet clothes I lay down on the bed. When I opened my eyes again I was aware of a bright, sunny morning, and the next thing I was conscious of was the warmth of Angel curled up on the bed next to me. Although I hadn't been asleep for long I was totally refreshed, and realised I'd slept better for those few short hours than I had at any time over the past two years. An even bigger realisation was that I was glad to be alive.

I got up and peeled off all my damp, dirty clothes. Angel was instantly awake and I was aware she probably needed to go outside, but first I needed to shower and dress. After an invigorating shower and much-needed hair wash it was great to have clean things to put on, and I silently thanked whoever had been so thoughtful.

I remembered seeing a ball of string in one of the kitchen drawers, and I used it to rig up an all-in-one collar and lead so we could head out for a walk. I was aware that I was thinking of 'we' and 'us' now rather than 'me' and 'I' which gave me great comfort.

How different the beach looked that morning. The tide was out, the sea was calm, the sky an endless stretch of blue. This was a beach I knew well, and pictures of deckchairs and beach towels filled my head again. I could still hear Amy and the other girls, their laughter and chatter, and I recalled being a part of it all – but how long ago it seemed. I wondered about Amy. Where was she? Had she graduated? Had she ever tried to find me? They would all have moved on by now and started high-powered careers, or gone abroad, or married. And here was I, left behind like the carelessly dropped litter on the beach, no longer wanted, but with nowhere else to go. I banished these melancholy thoughts from my head, and concentrated on the bright sunlight sparkling on the water and the little dog by my side. This was my life now and I must make the best of it. I had no family and no friends, apart from this tiny dog, but where had friends ever got me? Angel was probably the better option; at least she wanted to be with me.

I untied the string and let her run free, while I walked along with my hands in my pockets. I inhaled the sea air, let the coastal breeze dry my hair, and felt as though a calm had settled on me. I couldn't change what had happened and I couldn't bring my darling boy back, but I refused to allow myself to live in the past. I knew there was a way to move forward, and for the first time in as long as I could remember, I started to make plans.

Staying in the flat wasn't an option. I was fairly sure dogs weren't allowed, and even if they were, I felt as though I'd been put there rather than making an active choice to be there, and I wanted to take control of my life. One thing was clear in my mind, this little dog was going nowhere. She was mine now. Although I had set out to save her life, she had in fact saved mine, and I realised I was glad she had. So if this was a second chance it was up to me to make something of it. I knew I was an awful long way from being better, but I had taken the first steps towards it.

As I walked along the beach on that clear, sunny morning I started to think like the old Lydia. Nothing was impossible if you really set your mind to it, and no amount of mourning or guilt would change anything or bring my baby boy back. Deep down I knew I couldn't help what happened to him, it had been inevitable, starting with the traumatic way he entered the world and ending with the tragic way he left it. His father didn't want him and was set on getting rid of him – he'd tried hard to put an end to him before he was born. Whether I'd planned to leave or whether I'd stayed like a dutiful wife, I could now see that while Leo lived, the baby and I were likely to die.

This thought made me stronger, and I realised that all the time I was weighed down with guilt I had no fight and no chance of ever getting better. I felt no remorse for killing Leo, and if it all happened again I knew I would do the same thing. I only wished I'd done it sooner and saved my baby's life.

Later that day, after we'd gone back to the flat and had something to eat, the enormity of my situation hit home again. My earlier optimism deserted me. I had no money and no means of earning any, and no phone or computer – both vital tools for the jobseeker. Added to which, I didn't have a degree or any other qualifications, and had no idea who was paying my rent or for how long. On the way back from our walk I'd spent the last of my original £20 on dog food and a red collar and lead. So now I was penniless too. I looked at Angel and almost resented her for saving me, yet when she looked back at me with her tail wagging and her bright eyes shining full of love, I knew I must pull myself together. This was only the first day of my new life and far too early to despair.

It was then when I heard the soft tap on the door. For an awful moment, I was filled with fear; who was knocking? Had Leo somehow survived? Of course not, and if he had he certainly wouldn't bother knocking. Despite an almost overwhelming urge to hide, I forced myself to walk forward and open the door, revealing the smiling social worker who had brought me to the flat the day before.

'Hello, Lydia, I thought I'd give you time to settle in and… Oh my goodness, who is this little chap?'

'This is Angel, and she's a girl not a chap,' I replied. Thinking I sounded a little churlish I added, 'I'm sorry, I don't remember your name. Angel has sort of moved in with me; she doesn't appear to belong to anyone and she's good company.'

'It's Sophie – and don't worry, I'm terrible with names myself! Angel is very sweet, but I'm not sure you're allowed a dog here. I'll find out for you if you like.'

'No, please don't do that. No one knows she's here, she's clean and she doesn't make any noise, so nobody need know if you don't tell them. Please, Sophie…'

'Well okay, we won't say anything about her just yet.'

I think she sensed the panic in my voice and didn't want to upset me. I guessed she knew my background and was fearful I'd go 'mad' again. Then who knew what I was capable of?

Unlike Caroline, Sophie was a good bit older than me, and she had the appearance of a more motherly figure. Not that I'd had a mother to compare her with, but if I had I'd have wanted her to look like Sophie. She was no taller than me, yet quite a bit heavier, though without being fat. Her solidity was reassuring. Her hair was long, pulled back into a messy ponytail, and she wore little makeup. She had the air of someone who'd no time to spend on her appearance, favouring comfort over style. Her good quality branded clothes would have looked at home on a country walk. Tailored wool trousers, a V-neck wool jumper over a crisp white shirt, and a comfortable pair of lace up walking shoes, made her appear safe and trustworthy. Angel obviously felt the same way, as she fussed round her and demanded attention. So I decided I liked her.

'Anyway, I've brought a few things for you.'

As she talked she dipped into the large bag she'd brought in with her.

'We've applied for benefits for you, but in the meantime here is some cash to tide you over and a mobile phone so you are not cut off. I have already put my number in the memory so you can call me if you need to. I've also brought you a copy of the local paper and a laptop which you can use until you get on your feet again. Your rent here is paid for three months, but if you get a job or want to move away that's fine – you are free to do whatever you want to. I'm sure you already know your way to the shops, and you'll find the doctor and dentist at the Health Centre just off Kings Road. The building is set back from the road with a car park out the front, so you can't miss it. I've also brought you the prospectus and application forms for the new academic year at university; I think you probably know where that is. We've already established that in the circumstances they would be happy to have you back if you wanted to finish your degree.'

I was overwhelmed; it was a long time since I'd lived in the real world with real decisions to make. Last night I'd had no future, nor did I want one, but now, even though I knew I wanted a life, I couldn't think straight and didn't know what I wanted to do with it. I felt tears pricking the back of my eyes and had an almost uncontrollable urge to hug her. All the obstacles which had appeared insurmountable just a few moments ago had been swept away, and for the first time in months I could begin to see a way forward.

'I don't know how to thank you,' I said, resisting the urge to throw my arms around her.

'Ah, that's very sweet, but it really isn't me. It's my job and, that aside, I think you've had the worst possible deal in life. It's time you had some good news. Now is there anything else you need before I leave?'

I assured Sophie I had everything I could possibly need and saw her to the door. When I closed it behind her I gave way to the tears, but these were happy tears, and when Angel jumped up and put her paws on me to see if I was all right, I swept her up and danced around the room with her.

Now was the time for plans. The thought of going back to university was terrifying, yet also exciting. Could I go back? Could I really get my degree and become a teacher? The new academic year was due to start in about twelve weeks, but the application for a place and for grant aid would take all of that. If I decided to go, I would also need to earn some money, both before and while I was at university. The more I thought about it the more achievable it seemed. Why couldn't I go back? I was doing well when I was there before, and I really enjoyed it. I completed my first year and achieved quite good results, so hopefully I wouldn't have to do that again, but I didn't have any of my lecture notes or papers as they'd all been left behind in the flat. I realised I'd no idea what had happened to my belongings, and although I didn't want anything from my life with Leo, I would have liked some of my own personal things which I'd brought with me when I married. I would need to ask Sophie about these and perhaps I'd be lucky enough to get my notes back. Then I remembered that most of my work would be on the university portal, as this was where work was submitted and stored when I was there. I had no idea what they did when someone left. Did they automatically delete their work? I really hoped not.

I rushed across to the laptop Sophie had brought me, flipped up the lid and fired it up. After what seemed like an endless signing in procedure and verification, I realised I had no internet access, and that this was yet another thing I'd have to sort out. Feeling a little daunted, I picked up the mobile phone. I found an old and battered telephone directory on a shelf above a small table, on which no doubt a landline handset had once stood. I found the University of Brighton and, hoping they hadn't changed all their numbers, I scribbled down the one for enquiries. Then I realised I could have used my new phone to find the number, as it was a smartphone and appeared to have a good signal. To be on the safe side I did a Google search and discovered the number was the same as I had written down, so all good.

Then I sat down on the bed, phone clutched in my hand, and allowed all the doubts and fears to crowd back into my mind. What was I thinking? Of course I couldn't just pick up where I'd left off, I was a different person now: a wife, a mother – and a murderer. Everyone would know; my name had been in the papers. And none of the old crowd would be there. Everyone would be so young. No, I couldn't do it, it was a stupid idea.

Angel sensed my despair and silently hopped up beside me, fixing me with that intense stare I was beginning to recognise – the look that as good as said, "Pull yourself together; I'm here, I love you, you can do it". She nuzzled my neck and licked my face and I felt myself smile. Of course I could do it. I wasn't a victim, I was a fighter, and my life was worth living. With that, I dialled the number.

After speaking to someone on reception, I was put through to the Head of the School of Humanities, Jane Langton – a name I recalled. This came as a surprise. It seemed so long ago now, and I'd been sure everyone I knew back then would have left. Yet in reality it was only just over three years ago. She couldn't have been more friendly or helpful, and when I told her my name she remembered me too.

'Did you say Lydia, Lydia Carter?' I didn't correct her as I had no intention of ever using my Russian surname again. 'Oh how lovely to hear from you, and how good that you're coming back to us.'

'Well I'm only thinking about it at the moment,' I said. 'I was just trying to find out if it was possible, and if I would be able to access the work I'd done before online.'

'Oh yes, no problem, I can help you with that and walk you through your application. Why don't you come and see me – I'm sure I can persuade you to come back. You really were very good, Lydia, and you mustn't waste all that ability.'

I was completely taken aback, not just because she remembered me and was very kind, but also because she really believed I should resume my course. I made arrangements to meet her at the university later in the week. I would have gone the next day if she hadn't been busy, as I was worried that if I put it off too long I would lose my nerve. I was already wondering how I would cope stepping onto campus again. I pushed those thoughts to the back of my mind and decided that the new Lydia wouldn't be such a wimp. I stood up, squared my shoulders and lifted my head as if to prove how determined I was. I would be strong and I would go back to university. I decided to use some of the money Sophie had brought me to find a nice top to wear for the meeting, but now I would take Angel for our usual walk along the beach.

I was lost in thought as Angel scampered across the pebbles ahead of me and towards a man who was approaching. I looked up as he came closer, but as soon as he saw me staring he turned away and walked back up the beach towards the street. I only caught a glimpse of him as he walked, head down, with his hands thrust into the pockets of his hoody, the hood pulled up. I couldn't see his face, but there was something vaguely familiar about the way he moved, and his body shape. I felt uneasy, but had no idea why. Then, as he walked away from me up the beach, I suddenly knew. It was Leo! Oh my God, it was Leo!

I ran. I had no idea where I was going or what I was running from; I was overcome with terror and knew I had to get away. Angel was happy to run along beside me, probably thinking this was a wonderful new game, and I kept on running until I couldn't run any more.

Gasping for breath, I sank down onto the pebbles. Once again, Angel came to my rescue, licking and jumping up at me to bring me back to reality. Of course it wasn't Leo; Leo was dead; I'd killed him. I'd plunged the knife into him and watched the life go out of his eyes. No, this couldn't be Leo; but he was the same stocky build, and even with his head down he walked with Leo's sense of surety and arrogance, his back ramrod straight, that purposeful stride I'd learned to fear. It couldn't be him though, he was dead; it was my mind playing tricks on me.

I got my breathing under control and forced myself to walk back the way I'd run, until we were on familiar ground. There was no sign of the man, and I wondered if he'd actually been there at all.

Chapter 7

Matthew Benson woke drenched in sweat, struggling to breathe and trembling uncontrollably. This was nothing new, though it had happened less frequently of late and he'd been sure he was getting better. He instinctively reached out for the familiar hairy head and wet nose that always brought him back to reality at times like this. Then his heart sank; he remembered Midge had gone. The little dog he'd taken on a whim had turned out to be the one thing which helped him the most with his PTSD. But now he'd lost her.

He knew there was no point trying to get back to sleep simply to return to the world of landmines, bombs and waterboarding. It was already dawn and the light was edging around the curtains. Instead, he got up and made himself a cup of tea, decided he'd look for Midge again even though he knew in his heart it was hopeless. If the dog hadn't drowned she would have been found by now. He'd spent two days combing the shore, asking everyone he met if they'd seen her. But nothing.

Losing the dog was a blow to him for many reasons. The bad times had become far less frequent now, he was able to lead a pretty normal life most of the time, and he knew most of that was down to Midge. He was scared that without her the panic attacks and nightmares would return in full force.

At least with no close family he didn't run the risk of ruining relationships, or worse, becoming violent towards the people he loved, which he knew so many of his comrades had done. He had only himself to worry about, and he'd made good headway. He had a decent business in the bookshop in The Lanes, which had provided a sense of purpose and income since his aunt retired and asked him to take it on. Sadly, she'd died within only a few months of the handover, and he was both touched and relieved when he found out she'd left it to him in her will. So he was now a businessman, a man of means, and not simply a washed-up commando with PTSD.

As he sat at his kitchen table he started thinking about Midge again. Although scarcely grown, she had a wisdom far beyond her years, and had brought him not only comfort but a reason to get up every morning; a reason to go on. Within days of her coming to live with him, the nightmares had reduced, then finally stopped. Not only that, he'd not had a single panic attack since she arrived.

Even her arrival had been unusual. His aunt had turned up with her not long after he'd started work in the shop. She said she'd found her, and had intended keeping her, but didn't think it fair, as she wasn't able to walk her far, and – if she was honest – she found her a little too lively for her small cottage. She asked Matt if he would take her on and, although he'd never had a dog before, he felt immediately drawn to her. He never did find out the full story about where his aunt got Midge from, yet from the moment she came to live with him it was like she'd always been there. He agreed to have her on the condition he could change her name, as he couldn't keep calling her Snowy, which had been his aunt's choice. So he chose Midge, as she was quite small and very busy, darting around like the voracious hordes of winged insects that had all but devoured him when he was training in the Highlands. He took his responsibility seriously and realised she relied on him to be strong, and so, within a very short while, he was just like any other ordinary man with his dog.

But where was she now? He imagined her tiny body washed up on a beach somewhere and felt his throat tighten. The last he'd seen of her was her little white head bobbing up and down in the waves when she fell from the boat he'd hired for night fishing. He'd sailed up and down searching for her until morning, and had found and fished out the brown collar with the disc which verified she was his, yet he'd seen no sign of the dog herself. Perhaps she'd made it to the shore, but they had been a long way out and he doubted she could have swum that far. He realised now what a stupid idea it had been to take a young, boisterous dog on a night time fishing expedition with no lifeline or buoyancy aid. If he'd stopped and given it any thought at the time he would have seen the risk factors involved. Yet he'd spent the last five years of his life living with real danger, and nothing could have seemed safer than taking his little dog on a fishing trip.

Everything had been fine at the start. She sat happily on board the boat, with no sign of fear or panic. There'd been nothing in her behaviour to alarm him, right up until it happened. He'd gone over it in his mind many times over the last two days and had come to the conclusion there was definitely something strange about the whole incident. Midge hadn't actually fallen off the boat at all; it was as if, for no apparent reason, she had simply decided to jump off and swim for the shore. She hadn't shown any interest in the water until the moment she went over the side and, despite being almost within reach when she first went in, Midge made no attempt to get back on the boat. She simply swam away into the darkness, like a dog on a mission with somewhere she needed to be. Yet that was too mad for words. No, it was his fault, his stupidity, that had taken away his one friend and lifesaver, that had cost the little dog her life.

None of these thoughts helped his present predicament. He was frightened that the nighttime terrors would creep back, robbing him of sleep once again, and there would be no comforting head to stroke.

Matt realised he wasn't going to get back to sleep, and he had too much self-discipline to indulge in self-pity, so he decided to do what he always did when things began to crowd in on him; he went for a run. A 15K run, with his running playlist blocking out any chance of thought, always cleared his head. He stuck close to the shore, keeping his eyes peeled for the dog, stopping and running on the spot occasionally when he thought he'd spotted something, or to ask a passing dog walker if they'd seen anything or heard of a dog being found. As he arrived back at the flat, the sun now high in the sky, and Snow Patrol's 'Run' pounding in his ears, things seemed decidedly better. He might be blessed with another dog soon, or he might get a different life. Who could say? At least Matt had a life, and many of his former friends had not been that fortunate.

He felt invigorated from his run and planned to have a shower and get ready for the day, but it was still early and so he decided to sit and have a coffee first. The next thing he knew his coffee was stone cold in the mug, and he realised that not only had he slept, he'd had no bad dreams or flashbacks. He actually felt better; time to head off to work.

At twenty-eight years old Matt Benson was in good physical shape. Years of army training, which for the last five years as a commando had been extreme, had ensured his body was tuned to perfection; sadly the same could not be said for his mind. He'd always thought of himself as strong in mind as well as body, and had shown great strength and resilience after the death of his parents and younger sister in a car crash when he was seventeen. He'd been the only survivor. However, the action he'd seen and been a part of since had taken its toll, and left him suffering from flashbacks, insomnia and panic attacks.

Having never been one for academia, the army had seemed the best solution when Matt lost his family, and had in fact proved to be his saviour, providing him with a new family and giving him a purpose. All had been well until his last tour of duty in Kabul, which left him once again facing loss and bereavement; this time with the added horror of capture and torture. Even though his rescue was quick, he was left suffering from post-traumatic stress. Matt wasn't in a good place, and extended leave on medical grounds made it worse, as he could no longer face going back. He finally and reluctantly took the decision to leave the army; the only world he had known in his adult life.

Although he felt relief, it was coupled with a sense of loss, regret and guilt, and confusion and doubt about his future. That was when his aunt retired and asked him to take on the shop. Having lost her brother in the car crash, and with no children of her own, Matt was her only living relative. Although she realised he had no experience of running a shop, she was also acutely aware of his fragile state of mind, and felt a duty to her brother as well as a degree of self-interest in persuading him to take it on.

Even Matt was surprised how well this had worked out; he loved it. He met lots of people who were happy to chat with him – and who were equally happy to while away their time reading in the armchair next to the coffee machine – and he also got to read many amazing books himself. He couldn't believe that such a fantastic occupation could be described as work. It was perhaps a little too safe for a man with his background, but all in all he'd been content.

***

Then, that afternoon, he received a visit in the shop from his old commanding officer, Major Campbell-Morgan. Matt had a lot of time and respect for this man they had all known simply as CM. He had always led from the front, and even with the rank of Major and the double-barrelled name he'd remained one of the boys. It was really great to see him, although Matt was slightly embarrassed, realising he knew about his breakdown and the reason he'd left the service. He needn't have worried, as CM treated him no differently and made no reference to it. After exchanging pleasantries and establishing that he hadn't come to buy a book, he got down to the real reason for his visit. He wanted Matt to take on some work for the Military Intelligence Section 5 – or MI5. He explained that the work would be in Brighton, although he would have to travel to London periodically for debriefing and meetings. His role would be in connection with national security, including anti-terrorism, insofar as it affected that area of the country, and was part of a concerted effort to ensure MI5 eyes and ears were trained on all corners of the UK. CM said the shop was a perfect cover, because the work would be on a casual as and when needed basis. The reason he thought of Matt was not just because he was in the right area, but also because it was likely to be mostly surveillance work, an area for which he had a particular talent and for which he was well trained.

Obviously he would need help in the shop for the times when he was away, but the salary he would receive would more than make up for that, and he would be back serving his country again. CM also explained he was aware of Matt's medical history, but understood his problem was now well under control, and he truly believed, knowing Matt as he did, that this would be good for him.

Matt was astounded and excited. He felt the old rush of adrenalin – then practicalities kicked in.

'Thank you, sir, but I'm not sure I'm up to it.'

'Nonsense, Benson, it's made for you. I'll give you time to think it over and see if you can arrange the necessary cover. I'll be back next week for your answer; that should give you plenty of time to sort out practicalities and get yourself on board with it.' With that, he shook Matt's hand and left the shop.

When he'd gone, all the doubts flooded back in, yet with a new resolve Matt argued with himself on every point and started to believe he could do it.

The biggest problem would be the shop; if he had to go at a moment's notice it would be impossible to organise cover and he would have to close. Realistically though, he thought this was unlikely. From past experience he knew that any kind of surveillance operation took some setting up, so he was more likely to know well in advance. He started thinking about how to find someone who could come in and look after the shop, for anything from an hour or two to a day or two. Quite a tall order, especially when you didn't know anyone locally. Since coming back to Brighton he hadn't really made any new friends, although during his visit CM told him that one or two of his old army mates were now living in Brighton and Hove, and Matt made a mental note to look them up. He had lots of friendly customers but didn't think any of them would be looking for work. He'd met several dog walkers too, but none he knew well enough to ask for help. He realised this situation was of his own making, as he was wary of forming friendships for fear of losing them again. He was nevertheless pleased to hear he had comrades nearby, as they at least would understand. In truth, Midge had been the only friend he'd needed, but now she'd gone.

It was almost 5 p.m. when CM left, so Matt felt justified in shutting, although he was too restless to go home and too distracted to do any work in the shop. He didn't have his running gear with him or he'd have resorted to his usual mind-blocking routine. He opted for a walk instead.

Rather than turning towards home along the seafront, he went the opposite way, heading up towards North Street and the Pavilion Gardens. He would often run this way, but that was when it was late or early and virtually deserted. Whereas now, at just after five on a sunny evening, there were still lots of people around and the gardens themselves were very busy. Matt was drawn to these gardens whenever he was troubled, as this wonderful place never failed to lift his spirits.

When he'd first come home to Brighton, with his mind in turmoil, just sitting and taking in the beautiful surroundings brought him calm. It was early spring, and the scents filled his senses and soothed his troubled mind, delivering a measure of tranquillity which couldn't be matched elsewhere. The hawthorn blossom, lilacs and laburnum trees gave shade, and the purple broom, tulips, periwinkle and forget-me-nots provided a riotous burst of colour that dispelled both dark thoughts and dark memories. Now, in summer, the gardens were full of roses, peonies, hollyhocks and daises, and the glorious colours and heady scent once again filled him with a feeling of peace which allowed him to dwell on his present dilemma.

Matt decided a cup of tea would help with his thought processes. He made his way to the Pavilion Café, where he knew he would find not only a great cup of tea, but one of his favourite rock cakes – a speciality of the house. It always seemed wrong to Matt to refer to this wonderful place as a café, but he knew it didn't start out its life looking so grand. Matt's mother had taught him the history of the place when he was still a child, and he knew that during WWII, local entrepreneur Herbert Tennent was forced to close his seafront café to allow for the beach fortifications. Undaunted, he moved his business to the Pavilion Gardens, where his descendants still served the famous rock cakes Matt had known and loved since he was a boy. It was a constant in Matt's life, and it always made him happy when he paid the café a visit.

He took his tea and cake to one of the tables outside, and while fighting the seagulls for every crumb he turned his mind back to CM's visit and everything he'd told him. Gone now was the sense of panic; replaced by a feeling of excitement. He'd been seeing obstacles where there were none. He would find someone to mind the shop, and even if he didn't it wouldn't be the end of the world to occasionally close in the service of his country. He liked that thought, it made him feel useful again. Although he loved the bookshop, and was grateful for the new start it had given him when he needed it, he had to admit his life lacked a sense of purpose. It was beginning to seem a little too 'safe'. And the last couple of days the shop had felt so empty without Midge. It was as though it had been their joint venture, and it didn't mean as much now the little dog had gone.

He had no regrets about leaving the army, yet he sometimes missed the adrenalin rush before each mission and the knowledge that what he was doing actually mattered. Now here was his chance to do something meaningful again, and the more he thought about it the more he knew, whatever it took, he was going to do it.

Chapter 8

Over the next couple of days I settled into a routine: walking Angel, reacquainting myself with the seashore, checking out the local shops, rearranging the flat to suit me. I kept telling myself that seeing Leo on the beach had been simply a figment of my imagination. Of course I didn't see him; Leo was dead, and no one knew that better than me. I knew there must be lots of people who looked like each other. I would just have to get over it.

I looked for the man each time I went out, but when I didn't see him again I convinced myself I'd made the whole thing up. I regained control, and decided I would go shopping for that nice new blouse for my meeting at the university the next day. I changed into some clean jeans and a tidy top, gave the dog a bone-shaped biscuit treat and told her I would be back soon. Then I strode purposefully out of the flat, up the steps and into town.

It wasn't too long a walk, and I was bursting with energy, almost running when I reached Western Road. I loved being back in the hustle and bustle: people hurrying by; the exhilarating sights, smells and sounds of city life. Although I'd worried I would be out of my depth after being shut away from it all for so long, I was in fact anything but. I felt the smile spread across my face, and I wanted to run in and out of all the shops, try on all the clothes and soak up the atmosphere. And apart from the actual running, that's exactly what I did.

A little later, clutching more than one package, I decided to take a walk through The Lanes, the city's historic quarter with a fabulous maze of twisting alleyways. I'd always loved the narrow streets and brightly coloured artisan shops, and with my new life stretching before me I once again remembered the thrill of arriving in this vibrant city, recalled the day I found this magical place as a fresh and innocent eighteen-year-old. As always, The Lanes were packed with tourists and a good smattering of what were obviously students. The charm of the place would no doubt always be a draw to students, just as it had been to me when I first arrived.

Once the heart of the fishing town of Brighthelmstone, The Lanes were now home to a plethora of independent shops, offering a shopper's paradise of boutiques, gift shops, jewellers, sweetshops and antiques, as well as places to eat, bookshops, and shops which were too eclectic to label. All were bright and welcoming, and the smells and sounds were like no other place I'd been. A trip to The Lanes always felt like Christmas, even in the middle of summer, and it was possible to lose all sense of time – although I did suddenly remember Angel and knew I must be getting home.

As I turned to head back the way I'd come, I spotted the bookshop. Everything about it said 'come in'. I'd always loved bookshops, even the modern ones, but this wonderful old shop just looked as if it was full of treasures. Without a working television I had nothing to do in the evenings, and didn't want to spend too much time in thought. So perhaps a good book would be the answer, at least until I started uni again and had more important things to read.

The bell jangled as I went inside and the atmosphere hit me as soon as I entered. Warm and welcoming, like someone's sitting room, it was well-lit without being too bright. There were reading corners and comfy chairs set amid rows and rows of book shelves, and even the coffee machine was tucked into a corner so that it didn't spoil the ambience of what could have been a home library. Where to start? Then I saw the man behind the counter – a very attractive man I had to concede – totally engrossed in writing

some kind of notice with a black marker pen. Although the
bell had sounded when I entered, he was obviously someone
who believed in leaving customers alone unless they asked
for help, and for this I was grateful. However, I was short of
time and didn't know where to start, so I thought I'd ask if he
had anything new from my favourite author. Then I realised
I hadn't bought fiction for four or five years, and I'd been so
out of touch that for all I knew my favourite author might be
dead. I didn't want to look stupid, so decided to make a quick
exit and buy a magazine instead.

'I'm sorry, did you need some help? I should have
asked you sooner – if there's anything I can help you find
then I'm happy to do so.'

I was heading for the door, intent on making my
escape, and the question made me jump. I spun round to look
into the dark brown eyes of the good-looking man I'd noticed
when I came in, now standing right behind me, clutching the
notice he'd been working on. What was I thinking? Good-
looking man indeed! I knew all I ever wanted to know about
good-looking men; they couldn't be trusted. I made an effort
to appear casual and muttered something about being fine,
yet as I headed for the door once again, he spoke.

'It's this notice, you see. I don't really know what to
put. I don't want it to sound too formal, but it needs to look
interesting enough for people to bother reading it. Sorry, I
know this isn't your problem but there's no one else here to
ask.'

I thought this sounded a little desperate and certainly
not very flattering, as though I'd have to do in the absence
of anyone better. However, as he was obviously needing a
second opinion, I put my dented pride aside and held out my
hand to take a look.

HELP NEEDED was the heading, in big black
capitals, and then:

Shop help required on a casual basis, to cover

for the owner's occasional absences, and help out at busy times. Apply within.

It all looked fine, and judging by the discarded pieces of paper in the bin by the counter I guessed he'd had several attempts at it already. Like a bolt from the blue a thought hit me. I needed a job; I definitely wanted to earn some money before going back to uni, and even after that I'd still need some money coming in. Unless I decided to live on campus I would have to find a place of my own. Either way, accommodating Angel was not going to be easy. Then the devil on my shoulder asked me if I thought I could work with a man. Would I be too frightened? The more sensible side of my brain pointed out I would have to get over this irrational fear of every man I met, reasoning I'd have to work alongside men, or boys, when I went back to uni, so I'd better get used to the idea.

On the spur of the moment I put myself forward. 'Would I do?' I asked. Then, while I was still feeling brave enough, I plunged on. 'I've never worked in a bookshop, or in fact any kind of shop, though I did have a part time job in a café a few years back. I'm willing to learn and I love books, so would you give me a try?'

It all came out in a rush and I felt the colour creep up from my neck as he looked at me.

'Well there isn't really much to it. All the books are priced and categorised in a fairly simple and logical way. I only took over myself from my aunt a year ago and I'd never worked in a shop either, but I managed to grasp it. If you're willing I'd be happy to see how we get on. I'm Matt by the way.'

He held out his hand, and I shook it enthusiastically. 'Hi, Matt, I'm Lydia, and yes please, I'd love to try it out.' Then a thought suddenly struck me which changed everything. I was no longer a free agent. 'How often would it be, and for how long, as I have a dog? I don't have anyone to leave her with, and although I can leave her for a couple of hours in my flat, I would have to pop home if it was any longer than that.'

'Bring her,' he said, without any hesitation. 'I have... that is, I had a dog; she spent all her time in here, but...'

He paused, and I noticed him swallow as though fighting his emotions. 'What happened to her?' I asked.

He shook his head. 'Oh nothing... that is... well I've really missed her. So I don't mind another one coming in – although she's not a Great Dane is she?'

I laughed at the thought and assured him she was only a little dog. I could tell he didn't want to say any more about his own dog right then and I decided not to pry. He told me there was a small yard and garden with a bit of grass out at the back of the shop which was perfectly secure, and on nice days he used to leave the door open and his dog would sit out in the sun – so my little dog could do the same. He looked sad again when he said this, but I bit back my questions. We agreed I would come in for a trial and bring Angel with me. I told him about going to the university the following day and that I'd have a better idea of my free times and availability after that. So we agreed I would come in for a couple of hours in the afternoon and bring Angel with me. He commented on her name and asked me if she was indeed an angel. I laughed, told him that she was an angel to me and stopped at that. I said goodbye and left, but I was secretly pleased to see him tear up the notice as I closed the door, taking it to be a good omen.

As I walked home I glanced at my watch and was surprised to see how long I'd been gone; would Angel be okay? I needn't have worried, as when I got back to the flat and walked down the basement steps, I could see through the window that she was curled up fast asleep on my bed. As soon as she heard my key in the lock she jumped off the bed, greeting me at the door as if she'd been waiting there forever. I made a big fuss of her and fetched the lead off the hook before going straight out again. I figured it only right, as I'd been out enjoying myself, that she should have a good run. So we headed back to the beach where she could run to her heart's content.

As I climbed up the steps from the flat I saw the man again; the man I'd been sure was Leo. He was on the other side of the road, although with the garden area between us and the bushes running down the middle of the square, I wasn't immediately sure it was him. As I stepped up onto the pavement I could see him clearly, standing straight across from me. I could see it wasn't Leo; this man was taller and leaner. Nevertheless, there was an uncanny likeness which was unnerving. I wondered why he was just waiting there on the other side of the road? As soon as he saw me he turned and walked off, and when he came to the end of the square he went left and I went right. I didn't know why he made me feel so uneasy. Yes, he did look like Leo, but there were doubtless lots of dark handsome men around that looked a little like Leo. Was it something about his walk or his head carriage that reminded me? I wasn't sure what it was, yet I was glad to turn the other way and leave him behind. I reasoned that as I didn't know any of the residents in my street, or in fact anyone in the house I lived in, it wasn't unreasonable to suppose he lived in the square and was simply setting off out. I was being paranoid; it was my overactive imagination playing tricks on me. I suddenly remembered the Simon and Garfunkel song 'America' and decided he was a spy with a hidden camera. That would definitely be it: he was a foreign spy, loitering, waiting for an exchange of secret information, nothing to do with me at all. With that, I made myself laugh and we continued on our walk.

We stayed out longer than usual; it was a lovely evening and I really enjoyed watching Angel chase seagulls and splash in the shallows. I was pleased to see her late night encounter with the sea on the night we'd met hadn't put her off, and that she seemed in her element. I found myself laughing at her antics and forgetting everything else, so I was disconcerted to see 'the spy' again on the way home. He appeared behind me this time, and I hurried on and tried to forget he was there. I refused to start worrying about every man I saw, though when I got to my flat I couldn't resist a quick glance back. He was gone. I concluded my guess had been accurate and he probably lived in one of the neighbouring houses.

That evening turned out to be the best one I'd had since arriving at the flat. Filled with a new sense of optimism, I fiddled with the indoor aerial and managed to get a signal. I was able to watch the TV at last, although it wasn't the best picture in the world. I fed us both and then remembered the bottle of wine that had been left so thoughtfully in the fridge. Although I didn't wholly agree with drinking alone, I concluded that as I had Angel, strictly speaking I wasn't alone. So I allowed myself a couple of glasses. Suddenly life was good. I fiddled with the TV again and found it was also a radio, which meant I could tune in to some music. I found a retro station which played 80s music, and mellowed by the food, the wine and the dog as she settled herself beside me, I let my mind mull over the events of the day. I realised it had been a good one.

Chapter 9

The following morning I took Angel out for her walk much earlier than usual. There was no sign of the spy, and the day promised to be sunny and warm, so a good start. After our walk we both had a quick breakfast and then I went to shower and get ready for my very important meeting – or was it an interview? I was beginning to get nervous, and had to talk myself out of cancelling. I was dressed and ready much too soon.

My flat was about eight miles from the campus where I'd initially embarked on my degree. Although the University of Brighton is spread over four sites, with three in Brighton and one in Eastbourne, I didn't know much about the other three. I'd always considered myself fortunate to be based at the Falmer campus, right next to the beautiful Stanmer Park, and this was where I was going for the meeting. The downside was that it was a fair way out of town, but I'd done the research and discovered the 25X bus from Portslade came past the end of the square and would take me almost all the way there. I looked up my nearest bus stop and worked out I would need to allow around forty-five minutes to ensure I had plenty of time; at least I wouldn't have parking to worry about. This reminded me of my own little car and made me wonder what had happened to it. Although I'd done my best to blot out most of that last evening with Leo, I did remember walking past the Micra as I was helped out to the ambulance. I'd no idea what had happened to it after that. Something to put on my list for the next time I saw Sophie – if I was ever to see her again. Then I remembered that she'd put her number in my phone, so I made a mental note to either ring or text and ask to see her. I needed answers to the many questions which had occurred to me since our last meeting.

Checking my watch for the umpteenth time, I realised I still had at least half an hour before I needed to set out, and so decided there was no time like the present. Grabbing a quick cup of coffee I scrolled through my phone for Sophie's number, although it didn't really involve any scrolling as it was the only number there. I decided I must make the effort to find other numbers to put in there, perhaps starting with the bookshop. When I'd sent the text to Sophie and drunk my coffee, it was time to leave, so I patted Angel and told her I wouldn't be long, I let myself out and headed off to what I hoped would be the beginning of my new life.

I really enjoyed my journey back to uni. It had been so long since I'd been anywhere, and as I'd chosen to travel on the top deck of the bus I had a really great view. Everything was so familiar and I could almost imagine I was eighteen again, heading off to my new adventure. As we left the hustle and bustle of the town and took the road towards Moulsecoomb, I remembered how often I'd taken this journey in the past with Amy and Emily, returning from a day at the beach, or with Choy, Dusan and Will as well, on the way back from a concert at the Dome. Although the memories were clear and I could almost hear the laughter and feel the excitement, it was like I was remembering another person. In reality, I suppose I was; the eighteen-year-old Lydia had very little in common with the Lydia I was today.

As soon as I met Jane Langton again I remembered how much I'd liked her in my previous existence. I was both surprised and delighted when she brought some of my previous work up on screen and told me it was all still there. That was it, my mind was made up. Jane explained that as I'd completed and passed my first year, and she remembered me and could vouch for my commitment, she would recommend my acceptance for the second year of my course without the need for a new application to UCAS. Officially, with such a big gap, I should restart at the beginning, with a new application, but she felt sure in my particular circumstances she could persuade them to let me continue where I had left off. She promised to let me know as soon as she heard anything, but in the meanwhile she gave me access to the student portal and advised me to try to revise my first year, to avoid falling behind in my second. I left with a prospectus, a map of campus, lists of accommodation and a sense of purpose. Jane also gave me details of where to apply for the various grants, and I was pleased to discover I was still eligible for so much help. As I walked away from the campus I was as excited and full of anticipation as I'd been when I arrived there at eighteen. The interim years fell away, and I felt like the real me, the confident me, the invincible me. Before I met Leo I was always the optimist. I'd come to this place full of plans, with my future mapped out in front of me, proud as Punch to have 'made it' and determined to prove my worth. Little did I know what really awaited me, but that was all in the past, and here I was on the road to my future once again. All I needed now was an internet connection.

Then I saw him. The spy. Although he was still some distance away, I was certain it was him, yet as I made my way towards the bus stop, he disappeared behind the sports centre and was gone. I refused to let the sight of him spoil my mood. It was only his resemblance to Leo that caused my discomfort, and there was no need. I must have seen lots of people several times and never taken any notice. Why shouldn't he be at the university? It made sense that he would be either a student or a lecturer, as were a large number of the residents of this university city. Anyway he was gone, and there was my bus. I suddenly remembered my afternoon appointment at the bookshop, this time for both myself and Angel, and was once again elated.

As I got on the bus a ping on my phone announced I had a text, and once I'd sorted my fare and found a seat, I took it out to have a look. It was from Sophie, saying she'd be happy to see me and asking if I was free at 5 p.m. I checked my watch and saw it was only just after eleven. Even allowing for going home and picking up Angel I guessed I would be back from the shop by five, so I replied with a quick 'yes'.

I arrived home at around 11.45 a.m. and thought it would be wise to make myself a sandwich, as with the shop to go to and Sophie's visit at five I had no idea when I would eat again. I changed into more casual clothes, made a quick lunch and gave Angel a dog biscuit and my crusts. Countless foster parents, both friendly and unfriendly, had told me to eat my crusts, but now I could do what I liked, and it gave me a frivolous sense of power to feed them to the dog. Lunch over, we set off together on our adventure. A quick run on the beach to stretch her legs after being cooped up all morning and then a brisk walk into town. I strode out purposefully and even with her little legs, Angel managed to match my pace.

It was almost 2 p.m., and I guessed that could be counted as afternoon, so I made a beeline for the shop, feeling quite excited. As I opened the door, Matt looked up, and Angel gave an excited squeak and rushed inside, taking me by surprise and pulling the lead out of my hand.

Matt almost ran across the shop, much to my astonishment and that of the customer sitting in the reading corner.

'Midge! Oh Midge, I can't believe it – where have you been? How did you find me?'

And with that he dropped to his knees in front of Angel. She flung herself at him, licking his face and making a funny noise somewhere between singing and growling, her tail frantically wagging from side to side.

My heart sank; this was no ordinary meeting, this was a dog who knew her owner and an owner that knew his dog. I felt like a spare part as I watched the ecstatic pair, who both seemed oblivious to their surroundings and to me. I wondered whether I should leave, but I couldn't bear to walk away from her even though I knew she'd walked away from me.

Then suddenly Angel left him, swung round and jumped up at me, as if trying to include me in her homecoming; for that is undoubtedly what this was. I was angry, defensive and close to tears.

'If she's your dog, what was she doing swimming all alone in the sea at night and nearly drowning? You certainly weren't taking much care of her.'

It came out louder and more venomous than I intended, but it was the only way to fight back the tears.

Matt was immediately contrite. 'I'm so sorry, Lydia, it was thoughtless of me – of course... yes... she's your dog now, not mine. I lost that right when I let her fall in the sea. I'm just glad she survived, and she's obviously so happy with you; I wouldn't dream of trying to take her away.'

I too was sorry for my outburst; he couldn't help how he felt any more than Angel or Midge – or whatever she was called – could. Their greeting was spontaneous and natural, and no one could doubt their obvious affection for each other.

Matt was the first to recover, as I stood lost and alone in the middle of his shop.

'Come in, Lydia, come round the back and I'll make you a cup of tea, or coffee if you prefer. Bring Mi... Um, bring her with you.'

I did as he said. There was very little decision-making involved, I simply followed him as though I had no choice in the matter. Angel was completely oblivious to my mood as she danced around the shop, greeting the customer in the chair like a long lost friend, and then rushing into the back room behind the counter with obvious familiarity.

'Have a seat,' Matt said, gesturing to the soft leather

armchair that took up most of the space in the tiny room. He flicked the kettle on and asked what I'd like to drink. When I didn't reply, he answered for me. 'Hot, sweet tea I think – for the shock.'

I sat down in the armchair and Angel jumped up onto my lap.

'I still can't believe she's alive, please tell me how you found her.'

I didn't know what to say; the circumstances of Angel coming into my life were not something I'd allowed myself to think about since that night. However, I knew it would sound very strange to say I was walking on a beach in the early hours of the morning and decided to go for a swim. Just then, the shop bell jangled and saved me. While Matt served the new customer and said goodbye to the original one, I made a decision to tell him the truth. This was part of the new me – I wasn't going to hide or be ashamed anymore. I couldn't change what had happened, but I refused to get tangled in a web of lies. Here was a man I hoped to work for, so he deserved to know the truth. Although when I thought about it, I realised I probably wouldn't be working for him now.

Matt came back through, and I decided to seize the moment. I told him to forget the tea as I had something to tell him. Part of me was amazed I could talk so freely to this complete stranger, but then I reasoned that it was precisely because he was a stranger that I could. And if we parted company and I never saw him again, at least I would know I hadn't lied.

Matt listened; he didn't interrupt or ask any questions. I told him the whole sorry story, right up to the point when I decided this little dog had not only saved my life, but could also make my life worth living, and that's why I'd taken her home.

'Wow, no wonder you called her Angel,' was all he

said. After a slight pause, he continued. 'Of course you must keep her, and if you bring her to work at least I'll still see her from time to time. I can see she's happy with you and you with her – there's really something special between you.'

I couldn't believe that after all I'd told him about Leo, the baby, the mental hospital and the subsequent court case, all his concern was for the dog, and all the other stuff about me appeared to have gone over his head. I realised that somehow he understood how difficult it had been to talk about it all, and how close I was to breaking down. So he'd talked about the dog instead. Then it registered what he'd said about bringing her to work, so clearly he was still offering me the job.

He'd also said I could keep her, but realistically, when I allowed myself to face up to my situation, I knew this wasn't going to be possible. I wouldn't be able to stay in my flat once they found out I had a dog, and the student accommodation certainly wouldn't allow me to keep her. I couldn't really hope to secure an alternative dog-friendly rental on a student's grant either. I had to face up to the fact that finding Angel's owner was turning out to be a blessing in disguise, even though I couldn't bear to think of letting her go.

Now I'd started talking I couldn't seem to stop; none of these problems were Matt's but he was involved, so taking the bull by the horns I continued. 'I don't think I can keep her. I'll have to give up my flat and they won't let me have her in student accommodation, so you may have to have her back anyway.'

Matt was quiet and thoughtful for a while, and I wondered if he didn't want her back after all. Then what would I do? After a long pause, he spoke. 'Well after hearing your story, I think it's only right to share mine.'

Matt told me about his previous life, losing his family and joining the army. He told me about the tours of duty, the brief period of imprisonment and torture he'd endured, and then touched on the PTSD he'd been suffering and explained that was why he decided to take the dog. His aunt had obviously understood the situation he was in when he left the army and, at a time when she knew she would not have long to live, he was her perfect solution and she his. Then he told me about the fateful night when he lost Angel. He didn't make any excuses, telling it exactly as it happened, explaining how he'd searched for her, about the guilt and sadness he'd been feeling.

'So you can see why I was so happy to see her alive and well. Whether she is yours or mine doesn't matter, what matters is that she's here. I'm so glad you found her, although I'm sorry it was in the most terrible circumstances. Perhaps I was meant to lose her and you were meant to find her, because it seems she's done a wonderful job for both of us. So if you really can't keep her we'll sort something out. But if you're going to work here, how about living here?'

I must have looked confused, perhaps even a little alarmed, and he quickly continued.

'There's the flat upstairs, which you could have rent free. I stayed there for a while when I first took over the shop, and it's fairly comfortable, if a little on the small side. The dog lived there with me, so she's used to it as well. I have a flat in Regency Square, which I really wanted to get back to, so I moved out a while back. But I don't like leaving the flat here unoccupied, and would far rather have someone living in it. If you took it you'd be handy for the shop, and one of us would always be here with the dog. I don't think it would make the journey to uni any longer for you than where you are now, and there's a good internet connection, so you could do your online stuff here as well. It would be very useful for me to have you on call as it were, in case I need to go off in a hurry.'

I was quite taken aback. Here was the ideal solution; a solution where, although I had to share Angel, at least I wouldn't lose her, and I had somewhere safe for her to live.

'Well if you're sure, this could be the perfect answer to my current problems. It's actually closer to uni from here, and it would be great to know that Angel is safe when I'm not around. I do feel very guilty about leaving her so long on her own. Are you sure this is okay? Once I get my accommodation grant sorted I can afford some rent, or if you prefer I could work for free?'

'No need, the flat isn't doing anything or earning me any money now, so it won't make any difference. And if I charge you rent I'll only have to pay tax on it; knowing you and the dog are here will make me very happy.'

'Really, there's no need to keep calling her 'the dog'. If her name is Midge then I'll just get used to calling her Midge.'

'No, her name is Angel, and I will get used to that instead! She's proved herself worthy of the name twice now – once saving you, and in a different way saving me. So we'll keep calling her Angel, although you'll have to forgive me if I accidentally call her Midge occasionally.'

Hearing both her names, Angel jumped off my lap and ran across to him, as if to confirm that this new name suited her very well.

'Why don't you take a look around upstairs while I make that tea?'

When I stood up, Angel, as if understanding every word, ran across to the door at the bottom of the stairs to lead the way.

The flat was lovely, with quite a large kitchen and sitting room combined, which appeared to have everything I needed, and a lovely big window looking down on The Lanes. There was a nice shower room and two bedrooms. One was very small with just a single bed and a table, while the other was a decent size with a double bed and a wardrobe. Plenty of room for me and Angel – certainly a lot more than I had in my current flat. Furnished too, I could move straight in. I was thrilled, if a little worried that I was making some kind of commitment. Brushing this worry aside, I glanced at my watch and suddenly realised how late it was. If I left now I would barely make it back to my flat in time to see Sophie there at five.

I ran down the stairs and told Matt I had to go. I explained I had an appointment, but noting his worried face, I remembered to say I loved the flat and would come back the next day – as it had occurred to me we hadn't even spoken about the job. I wasn't sure what Angel would do when I left, would I have to drag her out or leave her there? But I needn't have worried, and I smiled as I went towards the shop door feeling the familiar little warm body against my leg. When I looked back, Matt was smiling too, so I didn't feel guilty taking her away.

Chapter 10

I didn't have time for a leisurely stroll back home, with Sophie
due at five, so I broke into a jog, and to my delight Angel took
it all in her stride, trotting along beside me like a seasoned
running companion. I couldn't help thinking she'd done this
before, and made a mental note to ask Matt about it. Our
run paid off, and I arrived back with time to spare and a few
minutes to settle before I heard the knock on the door.

When I brought Sophie in, Angel greeted her like an
old friend. However, I wasn't sure Sophie really appreciated
it; I decided she wasn't a dog person.

'Oh, I see you still have your little friend. Has anyone
complained about her?'

'No they haven't,' I said a little indignantly. 'There's
nothing to complain about; she isn't any trouble at all.
Anyway we won't be here much longer. I've found alternative
accommodation.' Thinking better of my rather unfriendly
tone, I quickly added my thanks. 'Not that there's anything
wrong with this flat, and I really am very grateful for all your
help, but I do need somewhere that will let me keep the dog.'

'Of course, I quite understand; is that why you called
me?'

'Well no, not really, as I didn't know I was planning
to move when I called you. A lot has happened in the last few
days and I have so much to tell you and ask you. Would you
like a tea or a coffee while we chat?'

I was pleased when Sophie accepted a coffee as I
really wanted one myself; it had been a long afternoon and
we never did get to that cup of tea at the shop. While I made
it I filled her in on everything that had happened. I told her
about going back to uni, and my job and flat at the bookshop.

I missed out the bit about Angel and her first owner, mostly because I didn't think she'd be particularly interested, but also because I wasn't prepared to talk to her about my trip to the beach that night. So far, other than me, Matt, and of course Angel, no one knew about my suicide plan, and I wanted to keep it that way.

As we sat on the two chairs with our coffee on the table between us, I got round to the main reason for my call, and asked her where my things were from the flat and what had happened to my car. She explained that they'd had no idea the car was mine, and didn't even know it existed until someone reported it to the police as abandoned. She told me the police had done a check and it came up as registered to Leo. This was news to me as I had no idea he'd changed the registered keeper to his name. She said the car had been taken to the police pound, and that as far as she knew it was still there. I remembered that the original documents were in my stuff at the flat, and they would prove the Micra was in fact mine, but I hadn't seen any of my personal things since I'd been led out on that awful night.

Although I hated bringing up the subject, and thinking about that night was almost more than I could bear, I forced myself to ask what had happened to my baby boy. She told me he had been cremated and his ashes scattered in the garden of remembrance at the cemetery. I decided there and then that as soon as I could afford it, I would place some kind of headstone or memorial in the garden. I would be the only one who remembered my darling boy, but at least there'd be something to show the world he had existed; that he was a proper little person.

Sophie then asked me about my things in the flat, and I was forced to try to remember what, if anything, I'd left behind that I actually wanted or needed. I could see by the look on Sophie's face that she found this deeply uncomfortable, and I realised that as she'd come on the scene quite recently, she would have been given only the briefest details of what had actually happened that night. She said she had no idea what had become of my stuff but promised she would do her best to find out, and in the meantime said she'd speak to the police about my car. I thanked her, and as she got up to leave I felt the need to say something more. I remembered her saying she thought I'd had the worst possible deal, but that was a huge understatement, and although I didn't want to go into all the details, for some reason it was important to me that I made something clear.

'I'm not a murderer!' I blurted out.

'Oh Lydia, I know you're not. I know your story and I know what you went through. Of course you want your stuff back – leave it with me and I'll do my very best for you.'

And with that she was gone.

I sat down on the bed. Why was it that any mention of that night put me straight back there as though it was yesterday? I felt shaky and nauseous, and I was gulping for air. Every part of me wanted to run. Angel came up and put her paws on my lap – did she actually understand? Could she feel my panic? More likely she just wanted her tea and a walk, but whatever the reason it brought me back to reality, and my emotions under control. I ruffled her head, stood up and set about getting our meal ready.

After tea it was time for our walk, and we headed off to familiar territory. We wandered on the beach for some time, and as was our habit we walked away from the centre of Brighton to the quieter end where there were fewer people. On this particular evening there was no one in sight, and it reminded me of the night I first encountered Angel on this same stretch of beach. Pushing those maudlin memories out of my mind, I thought about whether we'd still be able to walk this way when we moved. It was less than a mile from our current home to The Lanes, so there was no reason why not, and this thought made me happy. Then it occurred to me

I'd already accepted the fact that I was moving – surely one of the quickest decisions I'd ever made. So while I was in this positive mood, I made another; yes, we would definitely keep walking on this beach after we moved, as it made me feel warm and safe and familiar. The wrought iron bandstand just opposite Bedford Square gave us our bearings, and the blue railings which separated this lonely beach from the hustle and bustle of the Kings Road made me feel as though we'd entered another world every time we came here.

Then I saw him again – the spy – hanging around at the top of the steps. He wasn't going anywhere and he seemed to be watching me. I instinctively called Angel to me and slipped her lead back on. There was no logical reason for me doing so, only the fact that no matter how many times I told myself it was simply a coincidence, seeing him still made me feel uneasy.

Ridiculous – I was not going to allow myself to be intimidated. Recklessly, I turned back and walked towards him. I had no idea what I was intending to do or say, but as soon as he spotted me approaching he turned and walked off. By the time I'd climbed the steps he was nowhere to be seen, and determined not to have my walk ruined I went back down the steps and continued along the beach to the point where we had come down.

By the time we got home it was starting to get dark, so I flicked on the lights and put the kettle on. I still had the spy on my mind and was feeling unnerved. No matter how much I told myself it was all a coincidence, I couldn't remember seeing anyone else that many times, and was beginning to think there was something sinister about it. I wondered if I should mention it to anyone, but wasn't sure who. Having spent time in a psychiatric hospital I was concerned that anything I said to those who knew might be misconstrued as a relapse, and when I thought rationally about it myself I realised how paranoid it sounded, so I decided to keep my concerns to myself.

When I thought about my afternoon at the bookshop I couldn't believe I'd told Matt the story of my life. It was not something I would usually do, having learned at an early age not to give anything away that could be used against me. Yet I'd opened up and told my whole story to a virtual stranger. How weird. Perhaps it was because we'd only just met and I didn't care what he thought, but I knew this wasn't the case. I was going to work for him, so of course it mattered what he thought of me. Was it because of Angel? But I could have made up any story and told him I was simply out for a walk on that fateful night, yet I'd chosen to tell him the truth. I thought back to how he'd reacted and had to admit he'd taken it very well, his soft brown eyes showing only concern. Now what was I thinking? Soft brown eyes indeed. I dismissed him from my mind and went to make my coffee, wishing I'd thought to actually pick up a book while I was in the bookshop.

I'd promised to go back and find out more about the job the following day, but we'd made no arrangement regarding time, and I realised this gave me an opportunity to ring him, to see how he responded now he'd had time to think. I figured I would be able to tell if he wasn't keen, and although I knew he wouldn't be at the shop right then, the website for the bookshop gave a mobile number, so I decided to try that.

He answered almost instantly, and although he didn't immediately know who I was, when he realised it was me, he was warm and welcoming with no trace of hesitation or embarrassment. Feeling relieved, I made an arrangement to see him at the shop the following morning and told him I had nothing else planned so I could spend as long as needed finding out about the job. We parted on good terms, with him asking after Midge and then correcting himself to Angel, both of us laughing.

I felt better straight away. I was sure I was imagining things when it came to the spy, and I hadn't blurted out my paranoid thoughts to Sophie or blown my chances of a new job. As far as I knew I still had a new flat, a new job, and a solution to keeping Angel. I could relax, enjoy my coffee and look forward to my new life and whatever the future might bring. I looked down at the little dog gazing up at me and put out a hand to make a fuss of her. Without any hesitation she accepted the perceived invitation and leapt up onto my lap, nuzzling her head into my neck. I felt the smile spread across my face.

***

Matt smiled; his telephone conversation with Lydia had left him feeling inexplicably pleased. She was coming to the bookshop again the next day, and for some reason that thought gave him great pleasure. He told himself it was about seeing the dog, but even he knew that wasn't the whole of it. He liked her – really liked her – and after hearing her horrendous story and the matter-of-fact way she related it, he really admired her as well. Here she was, rebuilding her life and moving on. What a girl.

Then he returned to the other things he'd been mulling over before she called. Just after Lydia ran out of the shop that afternoon, CM had walked in, even though it hadn't been a full week since his last visit. He told Matt he'd completed all his other business in the area and had to get back to London, so he'd come for his decision – although thinking about it now, Matt realised he hadn't really come for a decision at all, it was more about filling him in on the assignment he'd lined up for him.

'It's to do with a known Russian operative called Viktor Kolocov,' he said.

Matt felt a rush of excitement: here was a real job, a proper mission, something he really wanted to do. CM explained that this guy was known to MI5 and was considered dangerous. The only possible reason for Kolocov entering the country was because he planned to eliminate someone, yet there were no Russian dissidents or asylum seekers who were likely to be targets for this particular assassin, and certainly none in Brighton. There'd been a younger brother in the UK, but he'd died, and they knew of no other family connection, so they really needed to find out what he was doing in the area. That was where Matt came in. They wanted him to carry out close surveillance work to pinpoint exactly what this guy was up to.

Something in the name Kolocov rang a bell with Matt, but he had no idea why – maybe it was a celebrity or footballer he was thinking of, as he didn't know any Russians personally. He took the details of where the guy was living and how to contact CM, and was given surveillance equipment, a mobile phone and several photographs. Then, after sealing the deal with a nip of Calvados from the bottle kept under the counter for special visitors, CM left. It was only after he'd gone that Matt really started thinking about what he'd taken on, and also whether Lydia would be able to cover in the shop for all the time he'd need.

Later that evening, it suddenly came to him where he'd heard the name Kolocov before. Lydia had told him her married name was Kolocov, but that she never used it now. He started to feel a little uneasy. Maybe there were lots of Kolocovs in Russia – perhaps it was like Smith – but he doubted it. The mention of the dead brother made it all the more worrying, and CM was clear that he was an assassin. Should he say something to Lydia, or would that just frighten her? He decided against it, reasoning it would be better to simply do as he'd been instructed, and find out exactly what Viktor Kolocov was up to.

Chapter 11

As I set off to the bookshop the following day, Angel trotting along beside me, I felt confident, positive and ready to prove myself. I'd decided to dress for work in case Matt wanted me to start straight away, and had gone for the smart casual look, with a white silk blouse and wide leg claret trousers, both purchased on my self-indulgent shopping spree. Because I was walking, I'd opted for comfort and wore trainers, but they too were a deep claret colour, so they looked pretty good. All in all I was sure I'd achieved the right look. There were a few people about as I walked, and for a moment I thought I saw the spy standing on the corner of Cannon Place. However, he'd already gone when I got there and so I put him out of my mind – after all, it could have been anyone, as I'd been too far away to see clearly.

When I arrived at the bookshop I glimpsed a look of relief on Matt's face before his smile of welcome; had he been worried I wouldn't turn up? But all that was forgotten watching Angel's ecstatic greeting, only slightly muted from that of the previous day. Matt once again dropped down to her level, impressing me with the ease of his movements. Then he looked up at me over Angel's head with the biggest smile, and we both laughed.

'Guess she belongs to both of us,' he said.

'Well I have no problem with that, as it means I don't have to look for a dog sitter,' I replied, grinning.

'Or pay for one!' he countered.

'Anyway, I'm afraid I'm going to drop you in at the deep end today, as I have to go out – but I do have time to show you the ropes and make you a cup of coffee before I leave. And we need to talk about wages.'

'And rent,' I added, hoping he hadn't forgotten about the flat.

'I told you, the flat is rent-free and I'm happy to pay you by the hour for your work in the shop.'

'Well that's more than fine with me and very generous.'

Matt grinned. 'You might not think that if you knew the hourly rate – but you haven't asked yet!'

'Ah well, I'm very out of touch and haven't worked for years, so you'd better just pay me the minimum wage, whatever that might be.'

Matt shook his head. 'I think we can do a bit better than that, but we'll see how it goes until the end of the week. Can you do a few hours today and tomorrow and then we'll sort it out on Saturday – and when would you like to move in?'

'Well I thought perhaps next weekend – the Saturday after this coming one – if that's okay with you?'

'Why not make it this Saturday, then we can work out your wages and get you settled in at the same time. No need to wait another week – have you got much to move?'

I realised I had nothing I couldn't fit in my rucksack, which was quite sad for a grown woman. Ironically, Angel probably had more gear than I did.

The next couple of hours were spent drinking coffee and discussing the shop and how it ran. It was really interesting learning how the books were categorised and priced. Not all had prices marked up on them, and it was necessary to refer to a ledger, where all the books were listed and crossed off when sold. Rather an old-fashioned system, and nothing was computerised, but I realised Matt's elderly aunt probably wasn't into computers, and guessed that most of the beautiful handwriting in the ledger – which went back years – was probably hers.

Once I'd got my head around how the system

worked, the rest was easy. Matt explained he'd been told by his aunt that the best way to effect a sale was to leave the customer alone. She maintained they knew what they wanted even if they weren't aware that they did, and left to their own devices they'd eventually find it. Hence the comfy chairs, drinks machine and soft music, all to relax the customer and make their choices easier. Matt said he'd been sceptical at first, but had soon found out that she was spot on, and most customers bought a book even if it took them over an hour to do so.

One or two customers came in while I was learning the ropes, and this gave me a chance to try out what Matt had taught me. I actually sold a couple of books, and was able to show a customer to the book he was looking for, so all in all I was pretty pleased with myself.

Then Matt said he would have to go. I felt a moment of panic, yet it soon passed and I told him I'd be fine. Angel had returned to what had obviously been her bed, and was curled up fast asleep. What to others may have looked like a linen basket with some rags in, to her was apparently heaven, and she was making full use of it. Matt said he would only be a couple of hours, three at the most, and would bring back some sandwiches for a late lunch. I gave him a wave and he went out of the door. I wondered what I would do between customers, as I hadn't thought to bring my laptop, thus wasting a chance to take advantage of the internet connection. Matt had told me to help myself to a book if I wanted to read, and it seemed too good an opportunity to pass up. What to read though? It had been so long since I'd read a book and I didn't want anything too heavy. Romance was out, murder was out, and despite my game with the unknown man I really wasn't into spies. Then I remembered what all the kids at school used to rave about. Back then I pretended I wasn't interested, but in truth I'd always been really curious about the young wizard and all his adventures. So I decided there and then that

I was going to read Harry Potter.

I realised I had no idea of the order of the books, although I'd somehow picked up that there were seven of them. Then I remembered my phone and so turned to Google for the information. It did strike me as funny that here I was, working in a bookshop, ready and willing to help the customers, yet I didn't know the most basic information about the Harry Potter books. Google didn't let me down, and listed all seven in order. The first one was called *The Philosopher's Stone*, and on checking the ledger I found that we had three copies in stock. I felt a sudden surge of excitement as I went across to the shelves and sought out the magical book. I was a grown-up and I was about to read a children's book, but it was my choice, I could do whatever I wanted.

I was interrupted only once, by a customer who asked if the book he'd ordered was in yet, and I was able to tell him from the paperwork I found that it would be there the following day. He went out happy, and the next couple of hours were spent getting to grips with owls, giants, Hogwarts and spells, not to mention walk-through walls; the time just flew by. Then the jangling bell made me look up, prepared with a welcoming smile. He stood there, staring straight at me; the Leo lookalike. And this close up, he really was like him. He walked right inside the shop, stood staring at me for a few moments, then turned around and went back out.

He left me rooted to the spot with the smile frozen on my face. The book had fallen to the floor, and for a minute I couldn't even move to pick it up. I could no longer believe it was coincidence; this man was stalking me, and studying him at close range, seeing the coldness in those eyes I recognised, I knew it wasn't because he liked me.

Yet no sooner had he left the shop than I heard the bell jangle again. I thought he'd come back and my heart banged against my ribs, but it was Matt. I felt such a surge of relief, and I realised how truly unnerved I'd been by the man's visit.

'What did he want?' Matt's voice was full of urgency, and I was shocked he'd realised straight away that he hadn't been an ordinary customer.

'I don't actually know; he just walked in, stared at me and walked out – but it's not the first time I've seen him.'

'What? What do you mean?'

So I told Matt all about my spy theory and he wanted to know when and where I'd first seen him. It felt like an interrogation, and I was uncomfortable, but as he realised this, Matt slowed down and suggested we went into the back for a cup of tea. I closed the Harry Potter book, using one of the bookmarks on the counter to carefully save my place, and then noticed Matt was watching me. He'd taken in my reading choice and was smiling, easing the tension. There were no customers in the shop, and true to his word Matt had brought sandwiches from the deli, so after a cup of tea we settled down to eat our late lunch and took up the conversation where we'd left off.

Once again I had no difficulty opening up to Matt, and told him about my first encounter with the man on the beach, how I'd thought he was Leo. Then all the 'coincidental' sightings since: around my flat, on the beach, and even up at the university. I told him I'd got over my initial fear and tried to treat it as a joke, making up the spy story so it didn't seem real. However, I had to admit that when he walked into the shop and stared at me it felt very real, and I was afraid. What was terrifying was that up close he did look exactly like Leo.

Matt stayed quiet and seemed to be struggling to find something to say; this was not a good sign. Did he now think I was delusional and paranoid? He filled the gap by offering me another cup of tea, and then the doorbell jangled and both of us jumped to our feet. Angel, convinced something was going on, also jumped out of her bed. The three of us were suddenly falling over each other in the small space, making us smile and once again breaking the tension.

Matt went back out into the shop to help the customer, who was struggling to find a particular book. He then became distracted by another he wanted to discuss, keeping Matt busy for a little while, and when he returned to the back of the shop Angel was on her bed again and I'd resumed my seat. He sat down, and then, as if he'd finally made a decision, he began to speak.

'I wasn't going to tell you about my other job, and I'm not supposed to – the Official Secrets Act and all that – but I think you need to know about this and no one else will tell you. You weren't far out with your spy theory – except that I'm a spy too!'

My instinct was to laugh, surely this was a joke? But when I looked at his grave expression I could see that it wasn't. 'What will no one else tell me?' I asked, not really wanting to hear the answer.

Matt started to explain, filling me in with all the details as far as he knew them, including the man's name: Viktor Kolocov. I felt a cold hand grip my insides and the almost overpowering urge to run.

He told me about the planned surveillance, and that the only places Kolocov had been were Bedford Square, where I lived, and then to the shop, where I worked. This was too much of a coincidence. Piecing all that we knew together, we were certain this man was indeed Leo's older brother, and the fact that he was a Russian intelligence operative probably had nothing to do with his visit to the UK – but the fact that he was an assassin may well have.

Panic was setting in and I started to gabble. 'I have to get away. I'll go back to Norfolk or up to London, or anywhere he can't find me. You'll have to take Angel, I'll just get on a train and disappear.'

'Whoa! Slow down, there's no need to run. I'm watching him, remember? I'll know every move he makes, and when you move in here I will stay and keep you safe. He won't get to you, I won't let him!'

We agreed I would move in the next day rather than wait until Saturday, and Matt would go nowhere, other than to watch Viktor, so he would never have the opportunity to get to me.

I knew he was trying to make me feel better, and part of me believed him, but all the fear and tension that had built up, and which I'd been holding in, was now escaping with long racking sobs. I was crying like I hadn't cried since the night I told my story to the lawyer. It was all so unfair; every time I got back on top of my life someone or something would come and knock me back down again. It had been the same all my life – moved from foster home to foster home without any thought of how I might be feeling. Then, just when I'd escaped and started a whole new life, Leo came along and took charge. Then my poor baby boy came into my head and I realised it had been the same for him; a helpless baby at the mercy of those who could determine whether he lived or died. And he'd died. Once again I'd made the mistake of thinking all of that was behind me. I'd started making headway, only to have to move and hide and live in fear again, just as I'd done my whole life.

I continued to sob, but I knew I must be a sorry sight and I tried to pull myself together – without much success. Angel left her bed and came over to try to console me and then, without another word, Matt knelt down next to my chair, took me in his arms and held me. I believed right then that both he and Angel would do their best to keep me safe. Although I hardly knew this man, I felt no threat or embarrassment, only a great feeling of comfort and warmth as I allowed myself to sink into his arms and finally stop sobbing.

At that very moment the bell went again. Matt swore. 'I'll get rid of this customer and close,' he said, and he got up and went into the shop.

I fished around in my pocket for a tissue, and set about trying to repair my face and regain control. I was aware that something subtle had changed in our relationship, but I couldn't worry about that now; it would have to wait.

Matt came back in, and true to his word he had shut the shop up early.

'Is there any reason why you can't move in tonight?'

'Well, other than some food in the fridge, Angel's stuff and my clothes, there isn't much moving to do, but I'm not sure if I'm allowed to move without asking my social worker.'

'You need to tell her, not ask her. Your own place is here waiting for you.'

'Thank you, and yes, I'd like to move here right away, you know that. Although it seems Viktor knows I'm here, so I may not be any safer.'

'Yes you will, I'll make sure you are. Now let's get back to your place and pick up your stuff. My car is in the car park, so I can take you there, and on the way you can call your social worker and tell her where you'll be. Mi... Angel, can come with us.'

Matt's slip made me smile; he was obviously trying very hard to remember the little dog's new name. Although I'd made up my mind never to be controlled again, I was actually enjoying not having to make any decisions, but I reminded myself to be careful not to slip into compliance. However, I knew in my heart I didn't need to worry about that here; this really felt like care rather than manipulation.

Matt said he didn't usually bring his car to work, preferring the few minutes' walk from his home in Regency Square – which I knew was somewhat grander than my square and closer to the shop – but he'd brought it in today as he'd had to go out, and so it was conveniently parked in The Lanes car park. All shop owners had a parking permit, and as we walked there, with Angel trotting along beside us, Matt told me I could use his permit if ever I wanted a car. I told him about the Micra and he said we must look into getting it back for me. His own car was a smart estate, and when he clicked the remote and opened the boot, Angel jumped straight in.

'Guess she's done that before,' I said.

'Yes, but unfortunately the last time was the night I lost her, and she was packed in there with a load of fishing gear. Doesn't look like she bears any grudges though.'

It took less than five minutes to get home and not much more than that to collect all my belongings. I telephoned Sophie on the way and told her of my move and my new address, but didn't tell her anything about Viktor as I thought she might think I was having a relapse. The good news was that she'd found most of my belongings from the flat stored away in a police vault, and she'd also discovered what had happened to my car. Apparently there was an extortionate recovery fee to pay to retrieve it from the police pound. She was working on that, and hoped she could get it cancelled. She said she'd drop my stuff off the following day, and expected to have news of the car by then too. As we headed back to the shop I started to feel better. Although Viktor knew where I worked, he wouldn't know I'd moved there – so at least I should be safe, even if only for a short while.

Matt helped me take my few belongings from the car park to the shop. I expected him to drop me off and leave, but he surprised me by suggesting we order a takeaway from the Italian restaurant around the corner. Looking at my watch I couldn't believe it was almost seven, and I realised that I was very hungry. Matt said he could highly recommend the house special pizza which – by his enthusiastic description – led me to believe he might be a regular.

I wasn't disappointed; the pizza was delicious, and Matt had ordered a bottle of wine too, so I was beginning to feel more relaxed – and in truth a little light-headed.

'I'm not scared of you, Viktor!' I suddenly blurted out with alcohol-fuelled bravado. 'You're just a bully like your brother, trying to frighten me – and I won't give you the satisfaction.'

Matt looked at me with a concerned smile.

'That's all very well, and brave of you, but you do need to take care until we find out what he's up to; he's a very dangerous man.'

'Yes, I know,' I said, feeling a little foolish. What on earth could I do to protect myself against an assassin? Who was I trying to kid?

'Well I'll stay here in the spare room tonight, and then tomorrow we'll get to the bottom of Viktor's intentions – even if I have to ask him myself.'

I told him there was no need for him to stay, that I'd be fine, even though I knew I'd feel far safer if he did. However, he said he still had a toothbrush and a change of clothes in the flat, as well as a sleeping bag, so he would be very comfortable in the second bedroom. I didn't put up much of an argument and we spent a pleasant evening discussing books and music and anything else which didn't touch on my present situation.

As we settled Angel in her bed downstairs and headed up to our own, it did cross my mind that his intentions might be less than honourable. I quickly dismissed the idea as unjust, as he'd never given me any reason to doubt him. Then the little voice inside me said 'and nor did Leo at the beginning'.

At some point in the night I woke to hear Angel growling before giving a couple of loud yaps, but she soon settled again. There were no other disturbances, and I felt guilty for thinking anything bad about Matt or his intentions. He was a good man.

Chapter 12

It would have to be today, there was no time left. He must kill her today. When he was called back to Russia he had no alternative but to go; it was a summons not an invitation. He must finish his business here without further delay.

When he'd woken up at his lodgings that morning he'd been instantly aware of a terrible headache. He got out of bed to take some pills and heard his phone bleep, alerting him to a text and when he unlocked it he discovered a curt message instructing him to report back to headquarters immediately. His initial reaction was relief; he could go home. He badly wanted to leave this awful country and put an end to this thankless mission, yet he knew he couldn't do so until it was complete. Checking the internet, he learned the first flight back to Moscow was that evening, so he booked a seat. That gave him the whole day to achieve his aim, then he could return home with a clear conscience.

The obvious solution was a sniper's bullet, and he berated himself for not doing it before. There'd been numerous opportunities to take her out, but it always struck him as being too easy. She would never know what hit her, and she would never know why. It was important to him that she realised there was a price to be paid for killing his brother and his nephew, but he was running out of time for the poetic justice he'd planned.

One way or another he would get the job done that day. He knew exactly where she lived, but when he'd followed her the previous evening he'd seen her go to her flat, then return to the shop where she worked with bags of stuff. He'd stayed there, watching the shop for most of the night, yet he hadn't seen her leave, so could only conclude she'd moved in.

Clearly she had another man in her sights now.

He'd actually ventured too close to the shop, causing the dog to yap. It could prove a slight hindrance to him, but the stupid thing was hardly a guard dog, so he wasn't too worried about it. Over the period he'd been watching her he'd learned that she was very much a creature of habit and – other than a trip to the university – she hadn't been far. She walked the dog on the beach, and now she'd got herself a job she also went to work. That was it. He would soon pin her down.

He started to plan, and realised that to get any sense of satisfaction at all he must think of a way of letting her know what was coming and why. No easy task with only this one day to do it in. He would have liked time to terrorise her over days or weeks before finishing her off, but this was a luxury he could no longer afford. Nevertheless, he must think of some way to intimidate and frighten her.

He grabbed his phone and changed the SIM; something he did regularly to ensure his cover. He'd managed to get hold of her mobile number with the help of a local sleeping operative – spinning a yarn about finding out he had a relative in the country and wanting to get in touch while he was here on a mission. The operative was no longer active, yet was kept on the payroll as eyes and ears, and as an aide to agents when they were in the country. He managed to come up with the number quite quickly and Viktor asked him to keep it off the record. The operative, who was flattered that Viktor had put his trust in him, was happy to oblige.

Viktor punched in the number and composed the text.

You evil bitch, I'm coming to get you. You won't know where and you won't know when, but I'll be watching you, and I'll decide when and how you will meet your end. Remember Leo and the baby you killed – you'll be seeing them soon!

He didn't sign it; he'd leave her to wonder. That was the first part of the plan in place. Let her worry about that.

He chuckled to himself; he might have little time left, but it was a good start.

Now to order flowers to be delivered; he would have to be more subtle here, as he didn't want to arouse the florist's suspicions with a threatening message.

Be sure I'm looking out for you. You may not always see me but I'll always be here xx

That should do it; an innocuous message which hopefully the florist would see as caring. Well he cared all right; he cared about finishing her off. He paid extra for same day delivery and requested the flowers arrive in the morning. He felt sure she'd understand the message's hidden meaning.

The next thing he needed to do was to check out his weapon. As a foreign intelligence operative, Viktor, like all agents, had safety deposit boxes in all the countries he visited. These were equipped with a change of clothes, a fake passport, local money, and a weapon, there for him to pick up when needed. However, the emphasis was on discretion, and for this reason he was not provided with the new SVC-380 Chukavin sniper rifle, which he would have much preferred for this job. He had to settle for the Ruger 57 handgun instead, which, although fully automatic with an impressive range, was still not the sighted rifle which would have made his job easier. He was aware of the availability of exactly such a weapon, and he could have contacted the sleeping operative again, who no doubt would have readily supplied him with one – but this would all take time, and that was the thing he didn't have anymore. He would have to make the best use of the weapon at his disposal.

He'd picked up the gun, cartridges and holster from his safety deposit box as a matter of course when he'd arrived at Heathrow. For him, strapping on the gun was as much a part of his routine as getting dressed; he felt naked without it. He'd also made use of the money, in the sure knowledge that once he'd put the gun back in the deposit box and left the country, it would be routinely taken care of; anything he'd used would be replaced.

He automatically checked the cartridges, but as he hadn't shot anyone since arriving in the UK, this was habit rather than necessity. Loading the pistol and securing it in the shoulder holster immediately made him feel in control. This was who he was: the cold, unemotional assassin.

Without the luxury of the sniper rifle allowing him distance from his victim, he would need to find a spot near enough to take the shot but well-positioned to make a hasty exit. He had no wish to get involved in a gun battle with the British police, or indeed to involve anyone other than his target, so picking the perfect place to carry out the shooting was very important.

Now the nagging headache had returned, and it was more intense. If he was honest with himself, there was a part of him which desperately wanted to return home without all this – but he owed it to Leo, and she had it coming, so it must be done.

He set off for the shop, hoping she'd be there on her own. He had to keep an eye on the time if he was to make his flight from Heathrow, so he couldn't afford to waste a moment. Annoyingly, he'd just had the text he sent her returned as undeliverable, so the number must have been wrong. You couldn't trust anyone to do anything right. Well, there was no time to correct that now, he'd just have to hope the flowers would do their job and that she'd be suitably terrified.

When he arrived at the shop, he bought a coffee in the café across the road and sat near the window. He would wait until he saw the flowers being delivered, then allow time for the message to sink in before finishing her off. He decided to do the job in the shop, as from what he'd seen it was never very busy. If she was there on her own it would be easy, as well as providing him with the cover he needed.

He had to buy another cup of coffee as the time ticked by without any sign of the delivery. Then he saw the flower shop van pull up and the driver take a bouquet out of the back. However, instead of taking them into the bookshop, he took them to the newsagents further down on the opposite side of the road. What was going on? This was the right van, and he was fairly sure the right bouquet, but the wrong shop. Did he give them the wrong address? He didn't think so, but looking across at the bookshop he now saw it was number 42, not 24 as he'd thought. He jumped up from the table and rushed outside, only to see the driver get back in the van with the bouquet and drive off.

'Dermo!' Shit! Now he was angry; first the text didn't get there and now the flowers. There was no time left to do anything about it, he would have to finish her off and that would have to be punishment enough.

He knew there was a customer in the shop, as he'd seen her go in. As the day was warm and sunny, she hadn't bothered to shut the door, and he could clearly see the inside of the shop. The customer was standing at the counter in conversation with his target, so he could probably slip in unnoticed and take up his position behind the bookshelves, where he'd be out of sight of the counter. He left his coffee on the table and moved swiftly across to the shop, in through the open door and round to the back of the middle bookshelf. He knew she'd recognise him if she saw him, so rather than cause a scene and have to chase her all over the shop, he decided to stay hidden and take the shot when she wasn't expecting it.

As he stood out of sight behind the shelves, she walked over to the table by the door and pointed out a book to the customer. He thought they might come round to where he was, but the customer was happy with the book she'd picked up and went back to the counter to pay for it. After another short conversation the customer finished her transaction, and as she left, his target called out after her, asking her to shut the door. This was a stroke of luck, as he didn't want to be disturbed, and it was likely that with the door shut no one would hear the shot. He moved position until he had a clear view of her.

The gun was loaded and his target was settled again now, tidying the counter; no time to waste, he must act fast. First, he ensured one last time that the coast was clear, then, breathing slowly and steadily to slow his heartbeat, he took the gun from the holster, stepped forward and took up his stance, lined up the target and... she moved. She was still at the counter, but had bent down, and was sorting something out on the shelves underneath. The door jangled and she stood up again, but before he could collect himself, a crowd of school kids walked in and quickly scattered themselves around the shop. He considered taking the shot anyway, but then thought better of it. It was too risky; what if he hit one of the kids?

To say he was frustrated was an understatement; she must have the Devil on her side, as she certainly had his luck. Viktor wasn't usually so righteous, he had become used to the fact that sometimes innocent victims got in the way of his assignments and paid the penalty for doing so, but he always drew the line with kids. He couldn't take the risk; he would bide his time.

He waited patiently for the children to leave, but a couple of them came across to the shelves where he was standing. He held the gun out of sight behind his back, though he was acutely aware he must look suspicious. Once they'd passed by, he returned the gun to the holster and glanced at his watch. It was already too late; he had to go. If he was going to catch the train to London and get across to Heathrow in time for his flight he must leave now. She would have to wait. He would be back.

Chapter 13

We were both up and about quite early and so had time for a leisurely breakfast. Matt had brought some provisions and we were able to make toast and a cup of coffee before venturing down to take Angel out. It was a great feeling walking down to the beach with Matt beside me, and Angel obviously enjoyed it too, as she kept turning round, looking from me to him and wagging her tail. Once we got to the beach, although she could run around to her heart's content, she kept coming back and circling us like a sheepdog, as if to make sure we stayed together. We both laughed.

'I guess Angel's life is complete, as we seem to be her two favourite people,' Matt said.

'Better not fall out then,' I replied, immediately regretting it.

'I wasn't intending to!' said Matt with a rueful smile.

Why did I say such a stupid thing? I hardly knew the guy and here I was imagining disagreements. I told myself I really must learn to trust my instincts and not think every man a danger – ignoring the pessimistic 'ah buts' and 'what ifs' in my head.

I decided there and then to let this thing, if it was a thing, run to its natural conclusion; neither fighting nor encouraging it, just allowing it to develop into whatever it was meant to be. As we walked along in companionable silence, I tried to think back and remember what I'd done wrong when I was first with Leo. I'd been all too ready to be flattered, grateful for the attention, eagerly agreeing with every step forward without thought or question. I couldn't remember ever asking myself if this was right for me, or if I was happy; I just went with all the wonder and romance of it, and refused to see beyond what I hoped it would be. Leo had driven our relationship and I'd been a willing passenger. This time, I resolved to say what I thought, explain how I felt, call a halt if things were not to my liking. That way, if a relationship did develop it would be on equal terms.

When we arrived back at the shop it was almost opening time and Matt asked if I could cope for a short while as he had some telephone calls to make. I assured him I'd be fine and he said I must call him if the 'freak' came in. I realised Viktor had gone from being my more lighthearted 'spy' to Matt's more sinister 'freak' in a matter of twenty-four hours, and that Matt wasn't joking when he told me I must call him. I wouldn't need reminding, as while I felt quite confident about managing the shop, I knew I would be terrified if Viktor came back.

Matt disappeared out back to make his calls, and in the absence of customers I resumed reading my Harry Potter which I'd left on the counter. I wondered if I should put some kind of cover on it so customers wouldn't know what I was reading. They possibly wouldn't take a bookshop assistant seriously who was reading a children's book, but I was enjoying it so much I wasn't prepared to give it up.

The door opened and a middle-aged lady came in and walked straight up to me at the counter. Unfortunately she didn't stop to close the door behind her, so although I shut the book quickly, I didn't quite manage to slip it under the counter before she spotted it.

'Oh, you're reading *The Philosopher's Stone*! Aren't they good? I've read all seven, and loved every one. They didn't have books like that when I was a girl, but you must be having a second read; I'm sure they were there for you.'

'Yes, but I never read them, although I always wanted to.'

'Well how lovely you can read them now, you really will enjoy them; my only regret is that there aren't any more.

Anyway, I'm looking for the latest T J Green book in the White Haven Witches series. Have you got it in yet? Oh dear, you will think me strange – from wizards to witches – but I love these stories.'

I was fairly sure I'd seen this book on display, so took her over to the new arrivals on the table by the door; and there it was. She followed me back to the counter and paid for the book, and after thanking me profusely she headed for the door. I called out to ask her to shut it as she left. She apologised for leaving it open, saying she was always so excited whenever she came in the shop, which was lovely to hear. My first sale and a ringing endorsement of my reading habits; not a bad start.

As soon as she left I started to tidy the shelves under the counter – I'd already learned that Matt could be a little untidy when things were out of sight – but I soon stood up again, as a crowd of noisy school children came in. They appeared to be running riot around the shop, although I soon realised they were just excited by all the books. I didn't mind, it was good to see the shop full, and a couple of them actually bought something. Their teacher was clearly pleased with their interest and varied taste, and it was apparent this was some kind of literary exercise. I thought that if things went to plan, and I managed to go back to university and get my degree, this could be me in a few years' time. I'd always wanted to teach English Literature, so what better grounding could I have than working in a bookshop?

The school children left, and shortly afterwards I glimpsed another customer leaving out of the corner of my eye. The shop was empty again, and as I resumed my tidying, Matt came back in and asked if I'd like a coffee. He'd finished his calls and I was ready for a drink, but really I was just pleased to see him, and almost said so. What was I thinking? Then I wondered if he thought I was taking advantage of him, paying me when he was there himself.

'You really don't need me to work today if you're here.'

'No, I know, but I'm enjoying your company,' he said, with that lovely smile which made me want to grab hold of him and kiss him. 'But, if you need to do something else, that's fine.'

'Well not really, but I could get things straight upstairs and then perhaps take Angel for a walk, if that's okay with you?'

We were boss and staff member, or landlord and tenant, and my moment of temptation passed, leaving me sounding stiff and formal. I felt sad about this, but had to admit it was me who'd forced the change of mood, when I could have replied that I enjoyed his company too. Instead, I chose to talk about doing something else, as if that was preferable to being with him. It appeared my guard was well and truly up again, and I was no longer that vulnerable, eager to please girl who'd fallen for Leo.

I hurried up the stairs to avoid any further conversation, Angel following me, yet rather than sorting anything out, I sat down, and she sat down too, looking intently up at me. What was I afraid of? Matt had never made any sort of approach to me and had behaved like a perfect gentleman. Our only intimacy had been a comfort thing – hadn't it? He probably saw me as a liability with all my problems and was simply trying to be kind. I realised Matt wasn't the problem, it was the way I was feeling that was scaring me. Even in these dark circumstances I'd enjoyed our closeness, the strength of him and, if I was honest, the raw masculinity and sensuality of him too. There, I'd admitted it; I fancied him rotten. Well that was my problem, not his, and I would have to deal with it. I heard the phone ring in the shop and it brought me back to what I'd come up here to do. In reality though, I had nothing to sort out. My few belongings made very little impact on the flat and I started to wish I'd brought my book upstairs with me. Then I remembered I'd planned to take Angel for a walk.

As I stood up I heard Matt calling me. 'Lydia, can you take over down here for a few hours please as I've been called in to work.'

Relieved to have a purpose again, I ran down the stairs and told Angel she'd have to wait for her walk after all. A thought struck me. 'Is it Viktor?'

'Yes, no need to worry though, as you can be sure I'll be keeping tabs on him. Although that's probably more than I should have told you.' Then he flashed that wonderful smile and my stomach turned somersaults.

I had a very quiet afternoon; only one customer, who browsed the books for over an hour before approaching me to buy three. Angel had given up on her walk and was sleeping peacefully in the box in the back room, so I was left to finish my Harry Potter. I was was scanning the shelf for the next one when Matt came back, grinning from ear to ear.

'He's going.'

'Who's going?'

'Viktor – back to Russia; he took a train to London and the Tube on to Heathrow this afternoon, and is currently waiting to board Aeroflot flight AFL49337 to Moscow.'

It took me a moment to register before I started with all the questions. How did he know? Had Viktor gone for good? Why had he gone? As well as many others which Matt couldn't possibly answer. He told me that when he'd called in to report on his afternoon's work he'd discovered a surveillance team had followed Viktor back to London and then on to Heathrow, and they'd established he was on the passenger list for the Aeroflot flight.

Although I hadn't said anything to Matt, I'd been worried that Angel's bark the night before had meant Viktor was prowling around outside the building – but now he was going, so it didn't matter anymore. I felt like bursting into tears. I hadn't realised how frightened I'd been, or just how much he'd been on my mind; the sense of relief almost took my breath away. I wanted to scream, cry, laugh, shout, all at the same time. It was as though I was going mad again.

Matt took one look at my face and put his arms around me. 'You're safe, it's alright, he's gone,' he repeated, as if talking to a small child. I clung to him with utter relief.

Later that night, as I lay in bed, all the fears and doubts returned. I felt on edge and couldn't sleep. So Viktor was gone, and I was safe. Why did I feel as if there was something I didn't know? I let my imagination run riot. Why would he leave without doing what he came to do? I started imagining letter bombs and poison, then realised how melodramatic this sounded, even to myself. Nevertheless, knowing Leo as I did, I couldn't believe Viktor would be so very different. I knew Leo would never forgive and forget, so why had Viktor given up on his intention, which was probably to kill me? Then I wondered if it was a ruse, staged to make us think he'd gone back. Perhaps he realised MI5 were on to him and decided to give them the slip by pretending to leave the country. Perhaps he was still here, outside, waiting for his opportunity? I could feel the panic rising within me and knew I needed to get control. Viktor had gone, I was safe, and I must keep hold of that thought.

Chapter 14

The following day I felt more positive. I spent the morning tidying the shop and returning books to their allotted places on the shelves. Matt had to go out for a few hours, which turned into the whole day. When he wasn't back at lunchtime I locked the shop for a few minutes and dashed across to the deli to buy a sandwich, which I ate sitting at the counter. Other than serving a few customers, I spent the afternoon with Harry Potter. I was now on the second book and knew there were still five more to come. I couldn't believe how lucky I was working in a bookshop and being able to help myself. All those years in foster homes, when nothing belonged to me and nothing was safe, meant the simple pleasure of knowing I could finish a book without the worry of being moved on was an experience which empowered me. I didn't need anyone to run my life or tell me where to be, and I certainly didn't need a man to control me.

Then Matt's face came into my mind, and the accompanying flip of my stomach warned me this was something I needed to deal with. I knew without a doubt that I was attracted to him both as a friend and as a lover, and this was worrying. The only other time I'd felt like this was at the start of my relationship with Leo, and look where that led. But Matt wasn't Leo, he was nothing like him. There was no arrogance or attempt to control; he encouraged me to do what I wanted, and the move to the flat had been on my terms and was my decision. I remembered Leo's insistence on making every decision, even down to how the furniture in the flat was arranged and how the contents of the cupboards were organised. I knew why he'd been so angry when I became pregnant; it was something done without his permission which was out of his control. That's why he wanted to end the pregnancy, so he could take back the control he believed he'd lost. But I had to stop thinking about Leo; he was gone, and I never needed to give him a passing thought again. It was Matt I should be thinking about. Then again, I didn't need to think about Matt either. I had no idea how he felt and there was nothing to make a decision about. What may or may not happen in the future was down to fate, just like other people's lives; there was no need for meticulous planning and going over all the 'what ifs'. The only thing I needed to be sure of was that I never relinquished control as I'd done before. I was Lydia Carter, and when called upon to do so, I would make my own decisions.

I'd finished my book by the time Matt came back, and when he asked if I'd been busy I felt guilty enough to confess.

He grinned. 'What do you think I do all day in a bookshop?' he asked. 'The most important thing is, did you enjoy it?'

'Oh yes, they're magical books, I can't wait to read the next one!' We both laughed.

'Let's go out back and have a cup of tea, and if no one comes in by the time we're finished then we'll close up. It's not far off five anyway.'

Matt made me smile again when he produced cakes to go with the tea. They had been in his rucksack, so the box was a little battered, but the fresh cream eclairs inside had survived, and were delicious. Then Matt went through to lock up the shop, and for the first time since that night on the beach I felt totally safe and content.

When he returned, we became aware of the eyes looking at us. Angel must have been wondering if one or both of us were ever going to take her for that walk. Matt had also taken the hint. He looked from her to me. 'Shall we?'

We all enjoyed the walk that night, no ghosts or

demons haunted us, Angel ran and splashed in the shallows, and Matt found a piece of driftwood for her which made her evening complete. I tried to remember if I'd ever felt so relaxed and at one with the world in my whole life, and the answer was definitely no. These two were the family I never had and the friends I had lost all rolled into one. Matt felt like my partner and Angel was like my child, but instead of fear and dread they brought me contentment and happiness. But I told myself I must stop thinking like that. Matt was an employer, a landlord, and hopefully a friend, and Angel was a dog. Time to come back to earth. As if to reinforce this, my phone rang, interrupting my thoughts.

I reached in my pocket and saw it was Sophie calling. Gesturing to Matt that I must answer, I took the call and discovered that not only had Sophie located all my personal stuff from the flat, she had also arranged for my car to be released from the pound. She would come and see me the following day. I ended the call not really knowing how I felt. Of course there would be things among my personal stuff I didn't want to lose, but I was terrified they would include baby stuff and other reminders of painful memories. The car would be useful, but I felt as though it had been sullied and would probably smell of Leo, so I wasn't sure I could ever get in it or drive it. All my earlier feelings of joy gave way to a feeling of heavy dread. It must have been written all over my face, as Matt came across and put his arm around my shoulders.

'Whatever has happened?' he asked, with genuine concern.

I told him about the phone call and how I felt. Even to me it sounded weak and stupid. I'd been talking about getting my car back ever since I knew it still existed, and surely anyone would be glad to have their things back, so how could I hope to make him understand how I felt? Yet somehow he did.

'It'll all be okay,' he said, as I pressed my face to his chest. 'You can sell the car and get another one, you don't even have to see it. I'll sort it out. Let me have Sophie's number and then text her to let her know I'll give her a ring. It's okay to drop the stuff round at my flat. You can come round when you're ready and decide what you want. I'll get rid of the rest. So no rush and no pressure – just when you're ready.'

I suddenly felt embarrassed, what kind of person gets in such a state over being given their own stuff back? I pulled back from Matt and looked up at him with a tear-stained face, aware I must look terrible. That was when he bent down and kissed me. It wasn't a friendly kiss or a comforting kiss, it was a kiss full of passion and desire, and I felt my own desire rise to match his and kissed him back with equal fervour. Then Angel jumped up between us, and the moment was lost as we pulled apart, laughing. Something had changed, and we were both aware of it, but nothing was said. We continued on our walk, and when I glanced over at Matt I caught him smiling.

***

Matt felt as if his head and heart were in turmoil. It had started the day Lydia walked into the shop, and if he was honest he hadn't felt quite the same since. The upside was that he hadn't had a single episode of night sweats or terrors. It was as though his PTSD had all but disappeared – which was unexpected in itself. But above all, he felt an overpowering need to protect this young woman, and he tried to tell himself that's all it was.

He'd never heard such a harrowing story as the one Lydia told him, and it almost made what he'd gone through fade into insignificance; perhaps that was why he no longer had to relive his own trauma in his dreams, as he now faced the stark reality of Lydia's story every time he looked at her.

There was no doubt she had killed her husband; she told him she had, and made no attempt to deny or excuse it, but he knew that if she hadn't done so, after what she'd told him about her life and the fate of her poor baby, he would have felt the need to do it himself.

With the arrival of Viktor, he'd felt genuine fear for her, a determination to keep her safe. Then Viktor had gone.

So what did he feel now? The sensible answer would be that he was her employer and landlord, and they had a good professional relationship. But he knew this was only part of the story; what he felt for Lydia was anything but professional, and what he'd felt when he kissed her on the beach had nothing to do with being either her landlord or her employer. No, this was something else, and it was time to acknowledge it. He loved everything about her: the way she looked, the way she moved, and most of all, the way she smiled. She'd been dealt a truly terrible life, which had gone from bad to worse, and yet she retained the ability to feel compassion for others – when she'd believed her own life should end, she immediately forgot about herself to save a dog. Watching her with Angel it was clear she still had the capacity to love and – judging by her response to his kiss – to feel passion. She was truly amazing and he was totally amazed by her.

Well, there it was: he loved her. But he knew she was vulnerable, wary and frightened of commitment; who could blame her? He would have to take things slowly and try to earn her trust. Of one thing he was certain, he would never give up on this beautiful woman who'd walked into his life and walked off with his heart.

***

When we got back from the walk, I expected Matt to go straight home; after all, Viktor had gone now so there was no need for him to stay. Instead, he followed me into the shop and put the kettle on.

'I thought we could do with a cuppa, and how about something to eat?' he said, taking me by surprise. I didn't think I could let him buy another takeaway, but I had nothing in so I couldn't rustle anything up.

'If you don't mind another walk then there's a really good chippy on the front; we could stroll along the promenade and eat.'

It sounded like a good plan. I couldn't remember the last time I'd eaten fish and chips. They somehow represented the carefree life I left behind when I married Leo, and they couldn't be any further away from the life I shared with him, so I readily agreed.

Angel couldn't believe her luck when after a quick cup of coffee we set off out again. Sadly for her, the walk didn't turn out as exciting as she'd anticipated. However, we really enjoyed it, and I felt eighteen again: in good company, without a care in the world. The food tasted really good and Matt made me laugh with stories from his army days, which although I realised must have been severely sanitised, were nevertheless very entertaining.

When we got back to the shop it was almost dark.

'Are you in a hurry, or would you like a cup of coffee before you go home?' I asked, feeling ridiculously embarrassed again. All the comfortable companionship had been replaced by an almost electric atmosphere, and when Matt entered the shop so close behind me I could almost feel the charge passing between us. Not bothering to turn on the shop lights we walked straight through to the back and up the stairs, and as I turned to ask what he'd like to drink he took me in his arms and kissed me.

I closed my eyes, emptying my mind of everything except for the feel and smell of him, and as my knees started to buckle he picked me up and carried me through to the bedroom. There was no resistance when he laid me down on the bed; everything felt right. I wanted him and I knew he wanted me. Our lovemaking was frantic and passionate, yet still imbued with all the tenderness I could have wished for. I'd never felt so loved, so wanted, so seductive, and I'd certainly never felt so much desire. Nothing I'd experienced before bore any resemblance to this awakening. It was as though I had never been made love to before, and when I considered it later it occurred to me that in truth I never had.

Gone was all the embarrassment, replaced by an understanding and mutual appreciation that went far beyond lust or opportunism. I knew, I believed we both knew, this was something special and this was how we were meant to be. There was no doubt and no conflict; I loved this man with every part of me.

Matt didn't go home that night, and neither of us got much sleep; we revelled in our new-found love and our new-found happiness, talking and making love until the light crept around the edge of the curtains.

We must have drifted off eventually, and I when I woke up it was to the smell of bacon cooking. I couldn't believe this man, was there nothing he couldn't do? Where did he find his energy, and more importantly where did he find the provisions?

'Full English or omelette?' he shouted through from the kitchen.

I couldn't ever remember being so happy. I had everything in front of me and a family to share it with; my man and my dog – but what a man, and what a dog.

Chapter 15

Life went on in much the same way for the rest of the summer. Matt hardly ever went home; we shared the days in the bookshop and the nights in my flat. He did go off on his mysterious assignments from time to time, but he never talked about them and I never asked.

His absences gave me ample opportunity to renew my acquaintance with Harry, Ron and Hermione, and I thoroughly enjoyed each and every fantastic adventure. I couldn't believe what I'd missed as a child, no wonder everyone was raving about the books at school. I had no regrets though, for discovering this world of wizards and dementors as an adult filled me with a childlike excitement which I'd thought was far behind me. Each new book felt like Christmas had come, but without the disappointment, which in the past had been so much a part of the season of goodwill.

As the summer turned to autumn it was time to start thinking about my future course at the university, so I put the fantasy away and turned my attention to reality. With Matt never sure when he would be called away, it was difficult for me to plan cover around uni. I felt guilty about this, as I would be leaving him in a muddle if I couldn't cover his absences, but he told me not to worry, his work was sporadic and sometimes he would go for long periods of time with no work at all. He said if he had to go when I couldn't cover then he would close the shop for the time he was away. It was never very busy, and now he'd finally got round to setting up a website, plenty of sales were done online, so he didn't feel the odd unscheduled closure would impact too greatly on business. I was always amazed the bookshop could keep going with everything now available online. It wasn't only books; whatever you needed could be bought with the click of a mouse. You would think shops like Matt's would have no place in the retail world anymore. However this was certainly not the case in The Lanes, which were always thronged with people. I knew this was far more about the experience than the purchases, though luckily one usually followed the other.

This reminded me I needed to go out and buy a few things myself, so I decided to start making a list. Just then, the lady who'd approved my reading a few weeks back came in and asked how I was getting on with the series. We spent several minutes discussing the various plots and Voldemort's evil plans, making ourselves laugh with our intimate knowledge of each and every detail. How wonderful to write a series of books which brought so many people of all ages together. I was in awe of the mind of the author who could bring such a fantastic tale to life.

My customer did eventually buy another of the witch books she clearly loved so much, and set off home happy. I wondered who she was going home to, or if she lived alone, and if her books provided both her entertainment and her company.

Although the bookshop was a magical place in itself, it was the customers who brought it to life, and since I'd been lucky enough to work there I'd met some really interesting people. I realised that all books, whatever the genre, brought pleasure to the people who bought them. It didn't matter if they were highbrow books, or what one of my rather saucy customers referred to as the 'fat filthys'. People bought books for so many reasons: some were used as time fillers, while others provided an escape, but there was no doubt that for some people, books eased their loneliness, provided company, albeit remote, and gave them something to look forward to. What a wonderful thing to be part of.

It was during this lovely summer that I ran into Amy

again. I'd taken advantage of a day when Matt was around in the shop to go out and get a few things ready for uni. Sophie had managed to get me some financial help, and with no rent to pay and a small wage from Matt I was actually feeling quite well-off. I decided I would treat myself to a couple more tops and some smart trousers. I was conscious of the fact I was still wearing the clothes which had been provided for me in my original flat and – other than the claret trousers and the top I'd bought on my first shopping trip – I had no others. I also needed some notebooks, a decent pen and a couple of highlighters, as well as some personal toiletries that I was running short of. With all this to do I expected to be gone some time, so after clearing it with Matt, I set off on my self-indulgent jaunt.

I'd been out a couple of hours when I decided to treat myself to a coffee and a cake, so I wandered into Pret a Manger in North Street. And there she was. I recognised her immediately, and it seemed she also recognised me. She jumped to her feet and almost ran across to greet me.

'Lydia? It is Lydia isn't it? I can't believe it. Where have you been?'

I was overcome with emotion, and I rushed forward to hug her. When we regained our composure, Amy asked me to go and sit at her table. 'I'll get us some coffee, I could do with another one for the shock. Do you want a cake? No, don't tell me, a latte and a blueberry muffin if I remember rightly?'

I felt a tightness in my throat and tears welling up, but I managed to laugh instead, confirming that a latte and a blueberry muffin would be great.

By the time she returned I'd decided I would tell her everything, but first I needed to know what she was doing in Brighton. She told me she was a teacher back in Surrey but she came to Brighton every year for the reunion – which was that night. Apparently the friends met up every year about this time, had a meal and a few drinks and caught up on old times. She said they would all be there tonight and why didn't I come, but I gave her a non-committal answer, for she had yet to hear my story. I was surprised to find there was no special man in her life, and laughed when I remembered it was her we teased on the bus about the number of boys she had waiting in line. She too remembered that day and started to giggle; it was just like old times. However, I knew the mood would change for the worse when I told her what had happened to me, so I put off the moment as long as I could by starting to eat my muffin.

But Amy refused to wait any longer for my story, and asked me again where I'd been – and where was Leo? I launched into my sorry tale, leaving nothing out and bringing her right up to date, including my relationship with Matt. To say she was astounded would be an understatement, and the fact that someone who normally couldn't keep quiet was rendered speechless gave full weight to her shock. Although I didn't want to make her feel bad, I did need to let her know how deserted and let down I'd felt when my friends started ignoring me, and when none of them ever tried to contact me.

Then she explained why. None of them liked Leo, apart from Will, and they all thought I was making a big mistake. Then I'd upped and got married without telling them and it seemed as though I didn't want to be friends any longer. This was borne out when Leo told them all I didn't want to mix with them anymore. He said I wanted to concentrate on my degree and felt they were holding me back, so I'd decided to keep away from them as I didn't think any of them would make anything of themselves.

For a moment I was astonished; how could he have done that to me? How could he have been so cruel as to ensure I lost all my friends? But then again why was I surprised? I knew how cruel he was and I should have guessed it was him who drove them all away.

Amy said she and Emily had talked about what Leo told them, and neither of them really believed it. They didn't like Leo, and certainly didn't trust him, so they discussed it further with the boys. To their shock, Will said they didn't know the half of it. Leo had told him some dreadful things I'd supposedly done and some awful things I'd apparently said about all of them; so they'd come to the conclusion I wasn't the person they'd thought I was. Leo never told any of them about the baby, but he did tell them I'd decided I wouldn't need to work so there was no point continuing with my degree. That's when they all finally decided I wasn't worth bothering with.

When Amy stopped speaking we went back to our lattes and muffins. There was really nothing more to say; we were both so shocked, yet somewhere deep inside us there was a recognition of the friendship we once had and the stirrings of a resurrection. We smiled at each other again, and it felt like old times. I decided I wouldn't go to the reunion that night, as it was still all a little too raw, and Amy understood. However, we swapped phone numbers and agreed to keep in touch on Facebook, and I said I hoped to be able to come the following year. Then we went our separate ways.

I felt a sense of relief. I'd never really acknowledged the effect that losing my friends had had on me, but finding one of them again and discovering the reason why they'd abandoned me felt truly liberating. When I got back to the shop I couldn't wait to tell Matt about meeting Amy. When I walked in he said he could see I was on top of the world, but he thought it was something to do with all the carrier bags I was holding. He was pleased I'd met up with an old friend and said it reminded him he still needed to catch up with his army buddies.

Later that evening I shared the information Amy had given me. When I'd originally told Matt my story in the back of the shop on that first day he didn't ask any questions. I was grateful for that then, but now, as we talked more freely, he said he'd always wondered what happened to my friends, and he could understand just how helpless Leo had made me. He knew I'd been happy at uni when I first went there, as that had been part of my original story, but I'd only touched briefly on the friends I had before meeting Leo. So now, with my new-found confidence, I went back to the beginning and told him all about my arrival at uni and the friends I made. I hadn't allowed myself to go back to those days very often, as it inevitably brought back memories of Leo and what followed, but now I found I could revisit my first months in Brighton without the pain. I knew this was not only down to this wonderful man, but also due to the fact I'd met Amy again.

When I told Matt about my trip down to Brighton in the Micra, about the fun times I'd had, he said he'd never seen me so animated. I couldn't remember ever talking so openly about my feelings to anyone before, and sharing the hopes and dreams which Leo had shattered brought them back to life. I would go to uni, I would make new friends and – most importantly – I would become a teacher.

Chapter 16

My first day back at uni finally arrived, and I was every bit as nervous as I had been on my previous debut. The sense of déjà vu made the whole thing feel surreal, but despite the familiarity, I also felt as though I was embarking on something new and exciting.

When I arrived at the campus for the very first time I found it overwhelming, yet now I remembered how quickly I'd settled in, and even years later I still felt that welcoming homely atmosphere and recalled exactly how much I'd loved it there. Although only a few miles from Brighton, the campus looked out over the beautiful Sussex Downs, and the modern buildings did nothing to detract from its rural charm. It was an enormous site with over 7000 students enrolled, and maps were handed out to show the way to the various classrooms, meeting rooms, lecture theatres and seminar rooms. The facilities on campus made it feel like a small town, where students could find most things they needed. There were clubs for just about everything too, and plenty of social life – which didn't interest me, but was obviously one of the big attractions for the newcomers.

Most students had arrived a week earlier to find their accommodation and get settled in with their new housemates. However, with no lectures for the first week, they'd clearly spent their time partying into the early hours and many were wandering around looking hungover or bewildered.

As I didn't live on campus, and I could remember my way around, I wasn't involved in all the rushing backwards and forwards, the clutching of maps, the looking lost. They all seemed terribly young and vulnerable, and despite their bravado, it was apparent that at least some were already feeling out of their depth.

One such lost soul was Hannah, and it was clear from the moment I set eyes on her that she was finding things difficult. She looked like a rabbit caught in the headlights, wide-eyed and wary, as though she might bolt for cover at any moment. She was a very pretty girl with long chestnut hair, which I later learned she spent ages straightening to prevent the wild unruly curls taking over. She was tall and slender with green eyes which – when she wasn't looking panic-stricken – were really beautiful and full of expression. I started off by simply smiling at her, and she immediately relaxed and smiled back, so I guessed she just needed someone to talk to. Over the next few days I got to know Hannah quite well. Despite looking so young, she had a wise head on her shoulders and a steely determination to succeed. She'd never been away from home before and came from what sounded like a very loving and supportive family. There was no late night partying for Hannah, and although she was living in a shared flat she obviously wasn't part of the crowd. She was on the same course as me, but was only in her first year. We therefore made natural companions, as being a year ahead of her I could help when she needed it. Within a short while of meeting her I knew more or less all there was to know about Hannah's life, but I didn't go into detail about my own. Although I did tell her about Angel, as she had left her own little dog back at home in Kent and was obviously missing him. She soon showed me all the pictures on her phone of her Border Terrier called Pip, and said she'd like to meet Angel one day. Hannah thought I was lucky living at home while attending university, and it was obvious that given the choice she would happily have forgone the student's social life to be able to study from home.

There were times when I envied the simplicity of Hannah's life. No succession of foster homes for her, and no disastrous marriage, but then I remembered that at her age the foster homes were behind me, and I too thought I'd finally found the simple uncomplicated life. How wrong could I have been?

Life settled into a routine, with lectures most days and also plenty of free time to study. And what better place to study than in a bookshop? Matt was really supportive and set up a desk for me in the corner of the shop. He was there a lot of the time, but when he went out on a 'mission' I could still get on with my studying whilst working in the shop. When Matt was there he was usually busy cataloguing books, and when customers came in, the very nature of their shopping meant it was mostly done in silence. So I remained undisturbed, and had the perfect environment to concentrate.

I had forgotten the simple joy of learning, and renewing my acquaintance with academia was both enlightening and enriching. As well as teachers, Falmer was the campus for nurses, linguists and social scientists, and I loved being among all these talented young people, and learning from them. Although we were all studying different things, we would come together in the dining hall or sports centre, or for social events, and while many conversations centred on the latest band or fashion trend, we also had deep and interesting discussions about meaningful things which affected us all. I'd really missed this interaction when Leo forced me to drop out, and being part of them now was both exciting and rewarding. When I allowed myself an occasional moment of self-pity, I regretted the time I'd lost, yet among these wonderful young people I felt humbly grateful to have been given a second chance.

This was, without doubt, the happiest period of my life so far. Matt was always there for me, and although some days he had to go out and some nights he had to go home, for the most part we lived happily as a couple. Our walks with Angel were usually taken together, and we shared most meals, so it was almost as though we were cohabiting. This arrangement obviously suited Angel well and she had become a content little dog, if a little fixated on time. She clearly liked routine, and we had inadvertently provided her with just that. Running the shop had forced us into a routine without either of us noticing it, and there was no doubt this worked well for Angel. She never troubled us during shop hours, but knew all her walk times very well.

I was pleasantly surprised how easily I picked up my course again, and although I was a year ahead of Hannah we could still talk through a lot of our assignments and essays, both gaining a great deal from each other's input. Yes, life was good, and as Christmas approached I felt for the first time in years that I would actually enjoy this one.

I was not disappointed. Matt and I decorated the shop together, and when we'd finished it looked like something out of a Dickens novel. We'd gone for the vintage look, and in an old-fashioned bookshop it really worked. Just looking at the finished project gave me that festive feeling. The shop was busy leading up to Christmas, and although Matt had to go out quite a lot, I'd broken up for the Christmas break so could be there all the time. Matt had rigged up a sound system so we were able to play carols, and I put out sweets in small bowls for any children who came in. For most of the year we didn't see children in the shop very often, yet as we got closer to Christmas it was lovely to watch them seek out their favourite books with great excitement. I couldn't help thinking we were looking at our future customers in the making, who would no doubt come and browse the shelves and sit in the armchairs in years to come.

On Christmas Eve, Matt brought in some wine and nibbles, and some of our regulars called to see us. It was lovely to hear them call me by my name and speak to me like an old friend, and Angel made the best of being allowed in the shop by greeting each one.

Although quiet, our Christmas was magical. I spent a

couple of days at Matt's lovely flat, and of course Angel came too. Matt had made a similar effort with the decorations there as well, capping it all off with a beautiful tree which filled the whole flat with the smell of pine. We made ourselves a delicious turkey dinner with all the trimmings, albeit with a turkey crown rather than the whole bird – but it still left plenty for cold snacks. We exchanged presents – just little things which made us both laugh – and we spent a good deal of the time snuggled up together on the sofa watching old movies with Angel at our feet, or sometimes, if she was lucky, on our laps. We walked on the beach every day, and when the tide was out we watched Angel splashing along the edge in the shallow water. We talked and laughed, forgetting the past and enjoying what we had here and now. Our days were full of loving companionship and our nights were filled with passion. Much as I loved my little flat, and enjoyed university and spending time with Hannah, there was a part of me that wanted to stay like this for ever.

When the new year arrived and the shop re-opened, it soon became time for the next term to start. I was happy to see Hannah again and hear all about her lovely Christmas with her family, and we'd only been back a week when she came to the bookshop and met Matt and Angel. This became a regular thing, and we often studied together in the shop on a Saturday afternoon, then she would join us for a takeaway in the evening. I think this stopped her being so homesick, and we all enjoyed it, especially Angel who'd adopted Hannah as part of the family. Matt was pleased I'd found some female company, and often left us alone on Saturday afternoons and took the opportunity to meet his old army buddies at last. He still paid me a regular wage for my help in the shop, although sometimes I wasn't sure I'd earned it. So on these afternoons, it felt good to really earn the money and to give Matt time off.

Life went on this way, and when the first signs of spring arrived I was as happy and content as I'd ever been.

Matt was still doing his MI5 work, but never talked about it, and in truth it had very little impact on our lives. When the Easter break arrived and Hannah went home for the holiday, he had plenty of time to spend with me.

Chapter 17

The shop only opened for half a day on Wednesdays, and on those days we got into the habit of going for a long walk with Angel after lunch. There was no doubt that Angel had stored this information in her brain. It seemed she could work out which day was Wednesday, because she was always bursting with anticipation on those mornings. It wasn't often that Matt couldn't make this walk, and we both really looked forward to it, but on one particular Wednesday during the Easter holiday, he was called away to London to meet the big bosses and learn more about a new top secret operation in Brighton. I wasn't really curious about it; he couldn't tell me anything and I didn't need to know.

I had an essay to write, so I was busy for most of the morning. One or two customers came in and I was able to help them find what they were looking for, but on the whole it was quiet, and by lunchtime I'd finished my essay and was feeling pretty pleased with myself.

As usual, Angel made it quite clear she knew it was Wednesday, and made me smile as she danced around, racing ahead of me up the stairs to my flat. Just as I reached the top, I heard a rattle on the door, as though someone was trying to force it open. I turned and ran back down the stairs, feeling slightly annoyed; surely they could see the closed sign on the door, and anyway what was so urgent about a book? As I went into the shop the man was turning away, so I dodged out of sight as I didn't want him to think I would open up for him. Just for a moment I thought it was Viktor again, but then he was gone and I chided myself for being so silly. Viktor was in Russia. I knew I hadn't yet put the past totally behind me; I still had the capacity to panic over imaginary threats. I made up my mind not to mention it to Matt, as everything was so perfect right now, and the last thing I wanted was to bring up the past again.

I would have a bite to eat and a coffee, then take Angel for her long Wednesday afternoon walk. Hopefully, by the time I got home again, Matt would be back and we would spend a lovely evening – and perhaps even night – together. The idea of it all made me smile, and I couldn't help thinking how comfortable we were with each other now. He could tease me without me feeling it was a criticism, and I could return the banter with no thought of saying the wrong thing. I suppose to most people this would seem normal, yet to me it was a revelation, and I knew this wasn't just down to my life with Leo. After so many different foster homes I'd learned the art of saying the right thing, of trying to please, from a very young age; this is what I'd brought to my marriage. No wonder Leo had been attracted to me. I was the ready-made obedient wife. But enough dark thoughts, I was happy and safe now and it was time to have lunch. I looked down at the expectant Angel and laughed. 'You'll just have to hang on for a bit girly; I must have something to eat and then we'll go.'

Although it was barely April, the sun was shining, and when we set out for our walk it was quite mild with no wind at all. I decided we should make the best of the weather and take the long walk up past the bandstand and on almost as far as Hove. Hannah was coming back the next day and we had a lot to catch up on. Once back at uni I knew there would be little time for walking, so I decided to make the most of the afternoon.

It was strange walking on my own again, as Matt had been with me all through the Easter break and I really missed him. It seemed Angel had no such concerns though, and as soon as we arrived at the beach she started running ahead and chasing the waves. Lost in the sheer pleasure of the silence and the beauty of the place, cut off from the hustle and bustle of the city, it seemed as though time had stood still, and it crossed my mind that for the first time in my life I had nothing to worry about.

I'd been taking life as it came since meeting Matt, but as I walked along in the sunshine I finally felt able to start thinking of our future, for I was sure we'd have a future. I allowed myself to imagine being married again, with a house of our own. Matt would no longer have to get back to his flat, and we would spend every night together and wake up each morning in each other's arms. Deep in thought, and with a smile on my face, I lost track of time and didn't realise how far we'd walked. It was time to turn around, and with a call to Angel I headed back the way we'd come. The sun was much lower in the sky now. I glanced at my watch – where had two hours gone? Matt would be back soon and here I was still wandering along the beach. I started to hurry, but realising I wasn't making much headway on the pebbles, I decided to head up to the pavement when I reached the bandstand.

The bandstand was an impressive structure styled on an oriental pagoda. Steps led down to a building underneath which was run as a café in the summer, but today it was deserted. The blue steps leading up to the street above were next to the bandstand, and came out opposite Bedford Square where I used to live. From there, walking along the pavement would be much quicker. I was really looking forward to seeing Matt, and also to Hannah returning the next day, and I soon became lost in thought again.

When I looked up to check where Angel was, my heart stopped. In front of me was Viktor. He stood up on the bandstand in the shadows and he was holding Angel in his arms.

I felt pure terror. It might as well have been Leo standing there; the old feelings of helplessness and inevitability washed over me. He was going to hurt me, he was probably going to kill me. But suddenly there was more than helplessness and fear, there was also burning anger. He sure as hell wasn't going to hurt Angel. I wasn't sure what I was going to do, or even what I could do, but I strode forward with my head up and my eyes blazing, shouting as I approached.

'Put that dog down! Leave her alone, she's not your dog. Let her go!'

When Angel heard my voice she wriggled and fought to get down, but he held her up and out by her collar and shook her until she stopped fighting and went limp. Then he tucked her back under his arm.

As I got closer, I saw the glint of the knife; he made sure I could see it as he held it at Angel's throat. There was no one else around, nobody to see, not a soul to help. I knew I could run, and perhaps stood a chance of reaching the pavement where there would be people around. Why would he kill the dog, it wouldn't help him catch me, and she'd done nothing to him? Then I remembered what happened to my previous little dog, and to my beautiful baby boy who'd never done anything to his father, yet it hadn't stopped him from throwing the child against the wall in anger. I couldn't take the same risk with Angel. It was running away which cost my baby his life; I wouldn't run again and leave this little dog to her fate.

I squared my shoulders and walked towards him. His position on the bandstand meant he was higher up than me, so I was already at a disadvantage. I refused to lower my head or appear servile; I wasn't that Lydia anymore. So, with my back straight and my head up, I walked forward. In my hand I clutched Angel's lead, trying to think of what I might do with it, at the same time realising the futility of the idea. What good was a little red dog lead against a knife-wielding assassin? Then it struck me, that just like my clothes on the beach, the lead would show I'd been there. So I dropped it at my feet.

When he spoke, in that same perfect English, in the same officious tone with the same sneer in his voice, I knew there wasn't going to be a happy ending.

'You won't give me any trouble, you will do as you are told. I will use the knife on this animal if you try to run or ask for help, and its death will be your fault; so come and walk with me and the dog will live.'

It was happening all over again. I heard Leo's voice declaring *I will cut up the baby!* and I knew Viktor meant what he said.

I stood rooted to the spot as he stepped down off the bandstand and joined me. Without a word he took hold of the bag I carried around my neck, opening it without taking it off me, almost strangling me in the process. He took out my phone, dropped it at his feet and proceeded to stamp it into the pebbles and cover the pieces. I was sure he would see the lead but he appeared not to notice it, leaving me with a pathetic hope that someone would be looking for me and at least know I'd been here. Then without a word he turned me around and pushed me towards the steps which led up to the pavement. With one hand on my elbow, and the other holding tightly on to Angel, he made me walk beside him. My heart was breaking as I watched Angel struggle in his arms and try to get to me. She whimpered and wriggled, but he let go of my arm and did the same hanging trick until she submitted and was quiet.

When we reached the pavement, he put his hand back on my elbow and ushered me across the road into Bedford Square. I remembered I'd seen him hanging around there before I'd known who he was, thinking he must live there; now it would seem I'd been right. However, he didn't go up that side of the road, but walked to my old flat instead, opening the gate leading down to the basement which had been my home. In one movement he shoved me down the steps in front of him and threw Angel to the ground, kicking out at her, yelling 'Vali otsyuda, vonyuchiy bomzhara!'

I had no idea what it meant, but the intention was clear, and although surprised, Angel still managed to dodge the kick and didn't hang about for another. The last I saw of her as I peered through the railings, now level with my head, was her tiny figure running down the road away from us with her tail tucked between her legs. My heart sank, and although I was glad she was safe, I felt so totally alone. I had twisted my ankle and scraped my knee when he'd pushed me down the steps, but the pain was nothing compared to the pain I felt watching Angel run away.

As Viktor opened the door and pushed me inside I saw that the flat was in total darkness, and when he flicked on the light I saw the curtains were not just drawn together but taped shut, and taped to the walls, so no light would be seen from the outside. In the middle of the living room was one of the straight-backed chairs, and on the floor close by were an ominous pile of ropes, rags and reels of tape. I knew from living there that the window by the steps was the only one in the flat with a view to the outside, and the only other form of light came from ceiling height glassed-in grilles, so there was no hope of help from that quarter.

Viktor grabbed my arm again, manoeuvred me towards the chair and then forced me to sit down. He didn't speak or give me instructions, simply pushed and pulled me around to where he wanted me, then proceeded to tie me to the chair with the ropes. Once he'd secured my arms and legs he pushed a rag in my mouth and taped another across my face, effectively silencing me.

He held a blindfold in his hands but then thought better of it and leaned forward to speak to me.

'We will not blindfold you, as Leonid and I want you to see us. We want you to see everything we're going to do to you and we want you to hear everything we're going to say to you. But we don't want to hear you, do we Leonid? Much as we'd both enjoy your screams we don't want to attract too much attention, so you must be silent.'

Viktor was insane. When I realised this I almost gave up all hope; he truly believed Leo was in the room and he was talking to him. I couldn't speak to defend myself, and Viktor had already condemned me. Together with the imaginary Leo, he intended to carry out the sentence.

Without another word to either me or Leo, Viktor calmly walked into the kitchen and made himself a drink. He came back, sat down on the bed, and looked as though he was about to speak, but instead he dropped his head into his hands. Without another word he rolled back and stretched out on the bed, and within a few moments he appeared to be asleep.

Chapter 18

Viktor had killed too many people to count. They were just jobs. There was no animosity towards the victims; there were no feelings of any kind. They were simply jobs to be done. He was a cold man, in control of his emotions, who truly believed that love was a form of weakness.

The closest Viktor had come to loving anyone was the way he felt about his younger brother, Leonid – who had also brought him the closest to feeling anger. Leonid had been arrogant, lazy and selfish from the day he was born, but Viktor excused all that, for here was a perfect boy in a loveless family who could be moulded into his clone. Unfortunately, as he grew up, Leonid had other ideas; he had no wish to follow his brother's guidance or career choices, he saw Viktor as dull and boring and he certainly didn't want to be anything like him. He knew he killed people for a living, as Viktor had always tried to convince Leo that this would be his own future too, yet although he was seduced by the power of taking lives, in reality he was squeamish. And it sounded dangerous. Of course he hid all this from his brother, as he enjoyed the attention and the company which neither of his parents bothered to provide.

Leonid played the devoted younger brother well, for exactly as long as it suited him. Viktor bought him things, paid for him to join clubs, drove him wherever he wanted to go. In return Leo pretended to enjoy Viktor's company and be interested in everything he did, but in reality he much preferred the company and attention of his friends, and of all the neighbourhood girls who thought he was exciting and fun.

When Leo was twelve, his father murdered his

mother; just another regular beating, but this one went too far. He received a life sentence. This didn't unduly upset Leo as he still had Viktor to ensure he got everything he needed, and he'd never been particularly fond of either parent. Viktor took the responsibility of his younger brother very seriously. Now he would be able to bring him up his way, with no interference from anyone else. Leonid would grow up to be exactly like him, to be his companion and his friend.

There were incidents when Leonid was a teenager, mainly centred around vandalism and theft, but there was also at least one case of sexual assault on a younger girl, and one of actual bodily harm against another. Viktor, with his connections, managed to get all the cases quashed with no records kept, and he put it down to teenage high spirits.

Yet all Viktor's hopes and dreams for his younger brother were shattered when, at the age of eighteen, Leonid announced he was going to England to study to become a teacher. To say Viktor was disappointed would be an understatement, but he held his emotions in check. He was trained to remain impassive, so he congratulated his brother and waved him off at the airport, then got on with his solitary life.

He heard nothing from Leonid after that; he made no effort to keep in touch and didn't even acknowledge his birthdays or Christmas. The first news he received was the news that Leonid was dead. He'd been murdered by a wife Viktor knew nothing about, alongside his baby son, whose existence was an equal shock. The news of his death came like a body blow to Viktor; at first he thought there must be some mistake and that this couldn't be his brother. His brother wasn't married and he certainly didn't have a son. But as the details came through, his devastation turned to anger and hatred – unfamiliar emotions, yet no less potent for that. Who was this English woman who had murdered his brother and his baby nephew? What sort of monster was she? Then he was told of her lies: her claims of self-defence, her stories of how his brother had beaten her and killed his own son. He knew then what he must do, and when he heard she'd been released, he decided to hunt her down and then kill her.

***

He had to smooth it over with work before he could take off for England, but eventually the day came when he finally set eyes on this evil woman who had no right to be alive. To begin with he watched her, as he did with all his victims; he needed to know how they lived and what they did in order to plan efficient killings. But in her case he was planning the most unpleasant way too.

It appeared to Viktor that Lydia Carter was simply getting on with her life; there was no sign of misery or regret. She had that stupid fluffy dog she appeared to dote on, and she obviously thought she could just pick up her life where she left off: visiting the university, finding herself a job. He vowed he'd soon put a stop to that.

He found out where she lived and who the flat was rented from, he found out who owned the bookshop where she was working, and he even discovered which course she had enrolled on at university. But she wasn't a woman to stand still; as soon as he'd pinned her down she was off again, moving her belongings to the flat above the bookshop. Work commitments back home were catching up with him, and he was running out of time to kill her. He had to put aside his ideas of terrorising her and move fast, but his last minute attempt to shoot her in the bookshop was also thwarted. He went home, determined to return in the near future, and vowing that next time he would have a concrete plan.

When Viktor returned to Russia he found he had a lot to catch up on. Post which had arrived in his absence had to be dealt with, bills had to be paid, and work had to be sorted. So, for a while, the return to England was put on hold.

It was during this period he started to see Leonid. The first time it happened he was at home. He was sitting at the table going through various bills and paperwork, when he realised he was being watched. As soon as he saw Leonid he knew he was disappointed in him for not having killed the woman yet, for not going through with the shooting when he'd had a chance. He tried to explain that he'd run out of time, that he had to return home for work, but he knew Leonid saw this as nothing more than a flimsy excuse. He promised him he would go back and do what must be done as soon as he was able, but Leonid had never been a patient child and he certainly wasn't a patient adult. Viktor knew he'd let him down.

As soon as he could, he shut up his apartment and told his bosses he was quitting. The Russian intelligence network didn't let people quit. They said they understood he'd recently learned of his brother's death, so they agreed in the circumstances to allow him extended leave, but left him in no doubt that he was still an intelligence officer and would be expected to return to duties within a month. He thought a month would be more than enough, so he set off for England formulating a plan in his head as he went.

Now here he was in the woman's old flat, which he'd had the foresight to rent on a short lease under a fake identity. It was easy to pass himself off as an English businessman, needing to stay somewhere near his work for six months, and the letting company didn't ask too many questions. He even managed to pass off the references he'd written for himself.

He felt a sinister satisfaction in his new plan. Bringing the woman back there would give him an opportunity to take his time over killing her, but also to let her lie undiscovered until the lease ran out, by which time he'd be long gone with no connection to the place at all. The flat proved very useful on his arrival as well; he'd spent a couple of days holed up there, getting together the things he needed, and waiting for an opportunity to strike.

It was while he was waiting that Leonid came back to him. Viktor knew Leo was pleased his brother was doing something at last, but he also knew he thought killing was too good for Lydia Carter. No matter how gruesome her death, it could never make up for the terrible things she'd done, and Leonid needed her to suffer and go on suffering for the rest of her life. Of course he was right, killing would be a mercy, but keeping her alive could prove far more satisfactory.

Then it came to him; or did Leonid suggest it? He wasn't sure, but he was sure he would approve. She had failed as a wife and a mother, so she would have to learn how to do it properly, and she would learn it in Russia.

After he had terrified her and inflicted maximum pain, she would be only too happy to comply with his new plan and return to Russia with him, to marry him and bear his children. He had no need for or belief in romantic liaisons, but he did need a dutiful wife to provide him with sons to continue his name. This was more important to him now she had killed Leonid's only son. It was her duty to provide a new heir. He would make her sorry every day that she'd taken the life of the only person he'd ever cared about. That would be far more satisfying than merely killing her. The more he thought about the idea the more he liked it. He was a man and he had needs; why should he pay for sex when he could have whatever he needed, whenever he wanted it, under his own roof? He could see Leonid nodding and smiling as he explained to him he would be using his wife for the family good. He felt no guilt; Leonid could see the poetic justice in his plan. Yes, this was the answer. She was not an unattractive woman, certainly better than some he'd paid good money for, and he would enjoy breaking her in to his liking. Leonid would witness every stage of her humiliation.

Now here she was in front of him, at his mercy. But

before he told her about his plans, he would have a little fun.

Viktor was almost happy, however he was also very tired. He'd had a headache ever since he'd landed at Heathrow, but – never one to make a fuss about illness – he'd simply carried on with the task in hand. He knew Leonid would not be happy with him if there was any delay, but the nagging pain at the back of his head was getting worse and beginning to make him feel sick. Perhaps he would lie down and rest before he started on her. After all, there was no hurry, no one knew they were here, and perhaps the waiting and worrying about what would happen next was a good enough punishment for now.

As soon as he closed his eyes, the nightmares started. He saw the faces of people he'd killed, coming for him, wielding knives, thrusting them into his head. The pain was unbearable. He couldn't fight them; he couldn't move; he had to get away; he had to stop the pain. He saw Leonid, telling him to get on with it, waving his fists, demanding that he make Lydia Carter pay. Then he too was sticking knives into Viktor's head. The pain was more than he could bear. Then there was nothing.

When he woke up the pain had gone and he knew exactly what he must do.

Chapter 19

Matt spent a very pleasant morning in London. His meeting with CM wasn't scheduled until lunchtime, but he hadn't told Lydia, as he'd come up early, intent on another errand.

He missed the early rush hour and travelled in relative comfort in a partially empty train. He picked up a paper at the station, and after catching up on the headlines he settled himself with the crossword, smiling inwardly as he thought of his big secret. Matt was going to buy a ring.

Although he wasn't yet sure of his timing, he knew he would be asking Lydia to marry him sometime soon, and he wanted to be ready. A part of him worried that she wasn't ready though, that he should leave it for a few months, but he also worried she would think he was taking advantage of her and had no intention of making a commitment. He had no previous experience of such things; what was the correct time? Was there a correct time at all? He knew things were complicated with Lydia. She'd been badly hurt and struggled with trust, but he was sure she'd come to trust him. He also knew that for him there was no doubt; he wanted to spend the rest of his life with her and he really hoped she felt the same. So he'd decided to buy the ring now, and then, when the time was right and he felt she was ready, he would be able to ask the question. He'd had no idea about the size, as Lydia didn't wear any rings he could use for comparison, but he had a brainwave and asked for Hannah's help. It had been impossible to speak to her in front of Lydia, so they made their plans on Messenger. Hannah agreed that the next time they went on one of their shopping trips she would get Lydia into a jewellery shop on the pretence that Hannah's parents were buying her a ring for her birthday and she needed help to choose. She was sure she could get Lydia to try some on too, then she would make a note of her size. With this subterfuge in place, they spent a Saturday afternoon in and out of jewellers trying on rings, and Hannah was able to not only determine Lydia's size but also her preference for sapphires. A cunning plan, and one he was quite proud of – he was now able to browse the London jewellers looking for the right size and the right stone.

Several shops and several coffees later, he finally found it; the exact ring he'd been looking for. A solitary sapphire set in diamond chip shoulders on a gold band. Understated beauty, just like Lydia. He was absolutely certain it was the right one. Now it was time to meet CM for lunch at his club and then go home to his beautiful lady and his wonderful dog; life was good.

CM's club was very grand, and although he'd taken trouble with his appearance and donned his military blazer and a regimental tie, Matt still felt underdressed. However, it seemed he passed muster, and he was shown into the inner echelons to find CM seated at a table waiting for him. Although he was now a bona fide member of the Intelligence Service he never went to the London HQ, and didn't even know where it was. Meetings always took place at some other location, and Matt supposed this was all in line with security. However, this was the first time he'd been to the club and he felt it was a step up. CM said they wouldn't talk shop until after the meal, so a leisurely couple of hours passed with good food, good wine and very good conversation, reminiscing about the old days with many a funny story and no reference to the darker times.

After they'd eaten they went into the lounge area for coffee and CM dropped his bombshell.

'I'm afraid your new assignment is a repeat of an old one. That Russian is back – you remember, Viktor Kolocov? It seems he's headed down to Brighton again. So I'm afraid you're back on surveillance duties, although we're as yet unsure of exactly where he is.'

Matt felt as if he'd been kicked. As his stomach turned somersaults, he regretted the heavy meal and the wine. He was hardly listening. He heard CM say he was at a loss to understand what the attraction was in Brighton, but Matt knew full well what he'd come back for and he also knew that the time had come to tell CM everything. He realised this might put an end to his short career in MI5 but Lydia was his priority now. CM listened intently and was equally as concerned as Matt. With no recriminations he told him he should get back to Brighton immediately and keep him apprised of developments. Matt was sick with worry and didn't need telling twice; with barely a goodbye he was up and away.

The train seemed to take forever to get to Brighton. Ever since CM told him the news, he'd been trying to contact Lydia to warn her. He'd tried ringing her countless times. At first he thought it was his own lack of signal causing the problem, but when his phone was showing four bars he was still getting no reply. What was even more worrying was that there wasn't even a ring tone. There was nothing; the phone appeared to be dead.

He tried to calm down, reasoning that Lydia may temporarily have no signal, or her phone may have run out of charge, yet at the same time he knew both were unlikely. All he could do now was try to get home quickly to make sure she was okay – his worrying could be for nothing. The train was full of commuters, intent on their own daily pastimes: some were reading, some doing crosswords, all in no particular hurry. Yet Matt could not sit still. He found himself pacing the gangway, much to the annoyance of his travelling companions. He checked the ring box in his pocket countless times, as if this concrete evidence of his love for Lydia would somehow keep her safe, even though deep down he knew something wasn't right.

By the time he got back to the shop he was frantic. He raced up to the flat to find everything in darkness: no Lydia and no Angel. It didn't look as if there had been any kind of struggle, in fact it looked as though they'd headed out for their usual walk. But it was quite dark now and far too late for them to still be walking. Matt faced the fact that they weren't coming back. He put on his hoody and headed out to look for them. He got as far as the beach and wandered up and down. There was no one around other than a couple of unsavoury characters near the bandstand. Matt decided that he needed to question anyone at all who might have seen something, so he headed over to ask them. He realised when he got there that it was unlikely they would be able to offer any help; he could see by their eyes they were completely out of it. As he turned to walk away he spotted the lead. Angel's lead, lying there on the pebbles. They had been here.

He wasn't sure if this made him feel better or worse, but he decided it wasn't a good sign. If they'd been here, why had Lydia dropped the lead, and where could they have gone where Angel didn't need to be on the lead? He knew Lydia wouldn't have left the beach with Angel loose, so he stuffed the lead in the pocket of his hoody and then walked up and down for the best part of an hour. He didn't find any other clues or see anybody at all, and so left with no options he headed back to the shop in case they'd come home. He wasn't hopeful. Then he remembered he'd given Lydia a key to his flat and decided it might be worth checking there on the way. It turned out to be a dead end, and he'd wasted more time, so he started to hurry back to the shop, hoping and praying she'd be there.

Sadly it was all still in darkness, no Lydia and no Angel, and it was now nearly 8 p.m. With his military training he'd learned not to panic, but he'd never had such an emotional investment before, and he was panicking. He contemplated phoning the police, but realised how this would look to them. His girlfriend had taken off with the dog and had only been gone a matter of hours. She wasn't a child, and the very fact she'd taken the dog made her an unlikely missing person. With more faith in his military connections he scrolled to CM's phone number and hit the call button. CM answered in a matter of seconds. When Matt had updated him he said he would contact a couple of other operatives and bring them down to Brighton to help co-ordinate the search.

Matt decided to stay the night in Lydia's flat; not that he had any intention of sleeping, but that's where he needed to be in case she came back. He realised he'd taken to pacing again when at 9.30 p.m. the shop telephone stopped him in his tracks.

'Hello,' said a female voice, 'you won't know me but I think I might have found your dog – at least your number is on her tag. Angel? There a was mobile number as well, but that doesn't seem to be working.'

Matt was suddenly elated. If Angel was there then Lydia couldn't be far away. 'Where did you find her?' he asked.

'She was sitting in the middle of the garden area in Bedford Square, where I live, and she'd been there for some time. To begin with I thought someone must be with her, but I couldn't see anyone about. I was sure she must be lost and someone would be looking for such a sweet little dog, but when it got so late and she was still sitting there I thought I'd better go and check on her. As you'll know, there's no address on Angel's collar, just her name and the two telephone numbers.'

Matt thanked her and said he would come round straight away, but when he'd heard where she'd been found his heart had sunk. Angel was obviously looking for Lydia, and being the clever dog she was she'd gone to the temporary home she remembered. But he knew Lydia wouldn't be there.

When Matt reached the address he'd been given it

was on the opposite side of the road to Lydia's old flat, and much further down, nearer the seafront. He was surprised Angel had been waiting so far away from where they'd lived. He would have expected her to be sitting outside the old flat if she was waiting for Lydia to appear. It was a little odd, but who knew what was going on in the dog's head?

When Matt arrived at the rescuer's door she brought Angel out to him. She went wild with excitement when she saw him. The woman said she had no doubt he was her owner and explained that she'd put her old dog's lead on her and he was welcome to keep it. He didn't have the heart to say he'd got her lead in his pocket, so he thanked her profusely and established that she'd at no time seen anyone with Angel. He promised he would take good care of her and left.

Once she had closed the door, Matt couldn't resist a walk up to the old flat, if only to convince Angel that Lydia wasn't there. The flat was in total darkness, so he guessed it was probably still unoccupied, yet as he turned to leave, Angel sat down firmly and refused to budge. How was he going to convince this little dog that Lydia wasn't there? He had no time for this, so he just picked her up and walked back to the car.

After a very long night pacing up and down and listening to Angel whine, he wasn't sorry to see the dawn break. After a black coffee, he set out on a run, but his real intention was to start looking for Lydia again. He left Angel at home, and when he got back, with no sightings and no clues, he could take no cheer from her greeting, which by her normal standards was lukewarm anyway. As he was starting to despair, and considering whether to phone the police, two things happened at once: he had a call from CM, and Hannah turned up. CM had nothing to report and was just checking Lydia hadn't come home. Hannah had arrived back from her Easter holiday the night before, and had come to see Lydia as they'd previously arranged. She was also hoping to get a quick glimpse of the ring she knew Matt would have bought by now.

Matt told her everything, as he saw no point in beating around the bush. In one way he felt disloyal to Lydia, as it wasn't his story to tell, but in order to understand the danger Lydia was in, Hannah had to know the full story. He needed her help.

Hannah was shocked, and Matt had to make her a cup of coffee and calm her down. She kept repeating that she'd known there was something wrong. She'd been messaging Lydia since the day before, and not only hadn't she responded but she could tell she hadn't even read the messages, which was totally out of character. Try as he might Matt couldn't think of anything to say to make her feel better; there was no possible good reason for Lydia's disappearance. He knew something very bad had happened, but unusually for him, he had no idea what to do about it.

Chapter 20

The fear I felt when Viktor Kolocov brought me back to my old flat was nothing compared to the terror which overwhelmed me when he started to speak. While he'd been sleeping I'd tried to think of ways to escape, but concluded there was nothing I could do. I was helpless, and no one knew I was there. Viktor moaned and shouted as he slept, so I was never sure if he was totally asleep or whether he would jump up at any moment. Now he was awake and that moment had come.

His voice, so like Leo's, was devoid of any emotion as he described his purpose and intentions. He didn't bother with the clipped English accent now, but spoke in a guttural, heavy accent, interspersed with Russian words I didn't understand. Although he told me he'd decided not to kill me, this was not in any way an act of mercy. He had a greater punishment in mind, yet he made it clear that killing me was not off the agenda if I tried to escape, made any sort of noise or refused to comply with his plans. If it all proved too difficult he would take the easier option and finish me off right there in the flat, where, he assured me, I would not be found for some time.

When he told me his plans my skin crawled. He explained he would have to overcome his revulsion for me in order to be able to 'mate' with me. He said he was finding this difficult to do, and he muttered under his breath. 'Zlaya grebanaya shlyukha!' Even without knowing what he was saying, his words were terrifying.

He said he would take me when he was ready, either in the flat or in Russia, but his first priority was to punish me, to cause me pain. As if to reinforce this he struck me across the face with the same brute force I had learned to expect from his brother. My eyes stung and I felt the blood trickle down my nose, yet I was determined not to cry or show any weakness. My resolve was all I had left.

Then things became more bizarre, as Viktor consulted with an imaginary Leo, asking him what he wanted him to do. He smiled and nodded in agreement in between each punch, each slap, each part strangulation, stopping from time to time to ask Leo if he was doing well. There was nothing sexual in his actions at this point, although he did have a disagreement with Leo about this, telling his ethereal brother that he wasn't ready for that yet. If it wasn't so terrifying it would have been almost funny.

Things took a more sinister turn when he started agreeing with Leo that it was all my fault – not only had I killed him and his son but I didn't even take my punishment properly. He asked if he should kill me and get it over with, but fortunately, in his mind, Leo didn't agree with that, so he resumed the random slaps and punches and kicks. Then, abruptly, he walked away.

He clutched his head and screamed at me, said I'd given him a headache and he would have to lie down. Without another word he flung himself on the bed and went to sleep again. He muttered in his sleep as before, but I couldn't make out the words, most of which sounded Russian. He slept for an hour or more, and I remained still, tied fast to the chair, rigid with fear and incredibly thirsty. I could feel my face swelling and one of my eyes closing, and I knew my nose was running, yet I could do nothing to stop it. I wasn't sure if it was broken but it was certainly very painful.

When Viktor woke, he jumped up and started rifling through drawers and cupboards, clearly looking for something.

'I need pills, have you got pills?'

I assumed he must be talking to me this time, but as I

couldn't reply there wasn't much point. He picked up the bag I'd been wearing around my neck and shook the contents out on the floor, though as he'd already thrown my phone away there wasn't much else to see – and certainly no pills.

He came across the room and stuck his hand in all my pockets, first in my hoody and then even more intrusively in my jeans, both front and back, nearly pulling me and the chair over in his efforts. My skin crawled as I felt his hands delving into each pocket. He struck me again and told me I was useless, walking back over to the bed, clutching his head.

Once again he lay down and fell immediately asleep, but I had no room in my head to think about his odd behaviour. I sat there, desperately thirsty, hungry, and in real pain. An even more pressing need was the toilet. I was terrified I would wet myself, which would be grimly humiliating. He started to mutter, and this time I clearly heard 'Leonid' and 'I'm sorry', and at one point he began crying.

I'd lost all track of time. I wasn't wearing a watch, as I'd taken it off to wash my hands before lunch and must have left it on the side of the sink. I knew there was a clock on the bookshelf behind me but in my present position, tied to the chair, I couldn't turn my body enough to see it. I tried to work it out but I had nothing to go on as it was completely dark and silent. Despite my increasing discomfort and terror, my body allowed me some respite. I dozed off sitting upright in the chair, yet what seemed like only a couple of minutes later I was fully awake again and nothing had changed.

I was cold. Although the day had been warm for the time of year, it was now really chilly and there didn't seem to be any heating on. Sitting so still for so long had made every part of my body ache, and I tried to flex my shoulders and stretch my back to ease my discomfort. Then the dark thoughts intruded, and I told myself it didn't matter how cold, how uncomfortable I was, or how much pain I endured, it was preferable to the alternative. He was going to torture and rape me, and if I didn't comply he would kill me. So at least the pain and discomfort meant I was alive. I really did need the toilet now, the pressing need was becoming unbearable, and I considered letting go. What would it matter? The only person who would know was Viktor. Who knows, perhaps it would help to put him off? No, I couldn't let that happen, it would mean losing all self-respect and everything which made me the person I was.

Positivity was needed; although I struggled for anything positive to think about. Angel knew where I was, perhaps she would bring Matt; but then I realised I'd watched too much *Waffle the Wonder Dog* as a child and these things didn't happen in real life. So it was down to me, I would have to formulate a plan. I would not be the meek, compliant victim, and I certainly wouldn't be going to live in Russia without a fight. If Viktor wasn't going to kill me, sooner or later he would have to take me out of this place. He no longer had Angel to use as a means of controlling me, all he had was the threat of violence, and I'd lived long enough with his brother's brutality to know I could withstand that. So that was my plan. I would endure what I had to until the day he was ready to move me on, and then, when I was out of the flat, and there were people around, I would scream and shout, kick, bite and fight to get away from this monster. I felt better, and in the words of Gloria Gaynor, I knew I would survive.

When Viktor woke up again it appeared the rest had eased his headache, and he announced to the room that he was hungry. He seemed to have very little interest in me; in fact he totally ignored me. As the time ticked on, he fed himself something out of a packet that looked like a pie or sausage roll. Then, after making himself a drink of something hot, he walked past me to turn on the TV. He returned to sit on the bed to watch it, and thankfully he continued to ignore me.

But then I was suddenly angry; how dare he behave

as if I wasn't there? Without the ability to speak, I couldn't reason with him or even make him aware of my basic bodily needs. I was boiling with rage, and I formulated all sorts of plans to kick him firmly between the legs if he came near me. As my feet were tied together that would be quite some kick, but then I remembered the rope that went around my calves and the chair legs, and I knew this wasn't going to happen.

Eventually, he must have realised I'd need the toilet, as he untied me from the chair, still without a word, shoved me into the bathroom and closed the door behind me. I tried to think of all my options but soon realised there were none. My hands were still tied, which was going to make using the toilet tricky, but he had undone my legs, so at least I could walk. There was no window in this room, and nothing in the cabinet. There was a lock on the inside of the door, but if I locked that it would only give me a temporary reprieve, as he would have no problem breaking the lock and I would achieve nothing except a possible beating. I used the toilet with some difficulty, but was thankful my legs were free, and using both hands to turn on the tap, managed to get a drink. Then the door was flung open and I was dragged out.

This time he didn't take me to over to the chair, but pushed me down on the floor next to the radiator and proceeded to tie me to it. Despite the falling temperature I was glad the heating wasn't switched on, or this would have been red hot. I really hoped he wouldn't start feeling the cold and decide to turn it on. My legs were bound together again and then tied to the pipe that came through the floor, my hands were tied in front of me. This time, in addition to the filthy gag, he did use the blindfold to ensure I was totally helpless, and he left me like this with one word: 'Sleep'.

I heard him walk across to the bed and the springs creak as he lay down. Then he started to discuss his plans for me with Leo, in conversational tones, as if he was indeed in the same room, ominously chuckling to himself from time to time. He was clearly deranged.

Thus began my first night of captivity with a mad man. I lay listening to him rambling on, until eventually he went quiet and then started to snore. I'm not sure how many hours passed but I didn't sleep, partly because I was too terrified and in pain, but also because I would not do as he told me. As he'd said 'sleep', I was determined to stay awake. I was now really cold and stiff, my movement was restricted to sitting up or lying down, neither of which eased my discomfort and no doubt contributed to my state of alertness.

I tried to think of nice things, and Angel came immediately to my mind. That little fluffy white head, her smiling face which had so often made me laugh. Would I ever see her again? Watching her run away had broken my heart, and worrying where she'd run to was equally upsetting. Then I thought of Matt, his dear face, his strong arms which made me feel safe and loved. What was he thinking? Where was he now? I wondered if he was out looking for me, but where would he look? Would he find Angel's lead? More importantly, would he find Angel? Too many questions without answers. Thinking about those I loved didn't make me feel better, it made me feel even more alone and desperate.

It didn't seem long before Viktor woke up. I heard him go into the kitchen, returning with what I presumed was a can in his hand, as I heard him pop the top and drink noisily. Then he came across to me. Kneeling down beside me, he must have put the can down on the floor, as now he ran both his hands over my body, grabbing at my breasts and panting like a dog. I felt his breath on my face and knew he must've brought his face down close to mine, but with the tape across my mouth and the blindfold over my eyes there was very little face for him to touch. He leant across and whispered in my ear.

'Ya dumayu, ya mog by yebat vas seychas!'

It hardly mattered what it meant, the way he said it filled me with terror. Then, as if wanting to ensure I understood, he repeated it in English.

'I think I can fuck you now!'

He pushed my top and bra up out of his way and manhandled my breasts roughly, pinching and squeezing. I was determined not to cry out. I wanted to bite and scratch him but my hands were tied and my mouth gagged. I had no defence at all. Then he unzipped my jeans and started to pull them down, despite my struggles. He shoved his hand down the front, but almost at once must have realised he couldn't do much with my legs tied together. I felt him move down to where the rope was fastened to the radiator, and then suddenly he groaned and fell. It sounded as though he got straight back up, but he was still moaning and crying.

'My head, my head, I can't do it Leonid, my head hurts too much.'

I heard him walk away, then the springs creak as he threw himself down on the bed again. Even without seeing him I could tell he was in a lot of pain; he didn't stop groaning.

I didn't think I would sleep, but I dozed off on the hard floor, with my top under my arms and my jeans down at my knees. I woke briefly and was acutely aware of my discomfort and the cold. I tried to use my tied hands to replace my clothing, which wasn't an easy task. I had more luck with my top than my jeans, but I pulled both together as best as I could and then slept from utter exhaustion.

Sometime later I was aware of Viktor whimpering like a wounded animal.

'I can't see! What have you done to me? I can't see!'

In a state of panic he got up, and I heard him stumbling around the room, threatening to kill me. He obviously couldn't remember where he'd left me, and I heard him knock the chair over in the middle of the room as he tried to find me.

'I'm blind, you she-devil, you're a witch. I'll kill you. My head! You're killing me with your evil!'

Although I couldn't see him, I could still hear him blundering about. He obviously reached the bed, as I heard the springs squeak again as he threw himself down. Then all was quiet until sometime later. This time I didn't sleep, but as I lay there I realised that with my hands tied in front of me I could, with a struggle, push the blindfold up off my eyes. The pain in my bruised face was almost excruciating as I did so, however, it was worth it, as now I could make out shadows, and could see Viktor illuminated by the moonlight which shone through the grille. He lay half on and half off the bed, and seemed more unconscious than asleep. I could hear his raspy breathing, so knew he was alive. I had no idea what was wrong with him, but I'd heard people talk of migraine affecting their sight, so assumed that was Viktor's problem. If that was the case, then sooner or later he would recover and the punishment would start again.

Another couple of hours ticked by. Without the blindfold I could make out the luminous clock on the bookshelf, and saw it was still only 3 a.m. I started thinking about Matt and Angel again. I knew Matt would be really worried, but he wouldn't know that Viktor was back, so would he think I'd left him? Surely he knew I wouldn't leave Angel, even if he didn't realise what I felt for him. What had happened to Angel? Had she got home safely? Had Matt found her? I really hoped she was safe; so many unanswered questions. For the first time since my ordeal began I started to cry. Alone on the floor, cold, hurting, with my stomach in knots from hunger and my throat like sandpaper, I still managed to produce tears. They stung my face as they ran down to my chin.

When there was a glimmer of light shining softly through the ceiling grilles, Viktor stirred. He jumped up, clutching his head, and I could see blood gushing from his nose. He fell to the floor, jerking and kicking, with his eyes wide open and saliva pouring from his mouth. He was obviously having some kind of fit, which lasted for a minute or so and then stopped. There was no more movement. His head lolled to one side, his eyes were still wide open, his tongue hanging out.

It was surreal, barely believable, but somehow I knew he was dead.

I was free... but would anyone ever find me?

Chapter 21

There was no doubt Hannah was deeply shocked by what Matt told her, and he wondered if he'd made the right decision. He really didn't want to spoil the friendship between her and Lydia, but he reasoned that if he didn't find her there would be no friendship.

Obviously distressed, and close to tears, Hannah spoke very quietly. 'What can I do to help?'

'I do need your help, Hannah. I need to go out and search, but I can't leave the shop. I could close it, but I need someone to be here for Angel and just in case Lydia comes back. So is there any chance you could hold the fort?'

'Yes, if that's what you need – I just wish I could do something more. I can't believe what Lydia has gone through. She never said anything to me about any of this, but I do understand why. She's so brave and we need to be brave for her.'

Matt was comforted by her response and glad he'd confided in her.

Although happy to be able to help, Hannah needed Matt to show her what to do. So, just as he'd done a short while ago with Lydia, he went through the basics. It wasn't complicated, and Hannah was bright, so she very quickly picked it up. He apologised for throwing her in at the deep end, but she told him not to worry, and said she would stay as long as she was needed and take good care of Angel. Matt had originally thought about taking Angel with him, but then decided that as she was already distressed and disorientated she'd be better in the familiar surroundings of the shop. He had no idea how long he would be gone, or even if he would need to travel somewhere else, so best she stayed safe with

Hannah.

He had daylight on his side now, and he knew Lydia had been on the beach near the bandstand with Angel at some point the previous day, as that was where he found the lead. He decided it was a good place to resume his search. He ran down to the beach, but was still scanning everything and everyone every inch of the way. He'd been trained to pick out one face in a crowd, and hoped he might spot Lydia or Viktor, or both of them together, yet realistically he knew this was very unlikely. He returned to the spot where he'd found the lead, as this was the last concrete piece of evidence he had, but staring down at the pebbles didn't really provide him with any more information, until... what was that glinting...? He bent to scrape the pebbles away and found enough pieces of smashed phone to recognise it as Lydia's. His blood ran cold.

Okay, Lydia had been here, and the likelihood was that the dog had been here too, but Angel was found across the road in Bedford Square. Did she run there because it was a place she knew? If that was the case she'd done well not to get run over, as the Kings Road was always very busy. Where did Viktor take Lydia? For Matt had no doubt that Viktor had taken her. Or had he already killed her? He was an assassin after all, and he wouldn't waste time. He knew how to kill, and he knew how to get away. Matt was becoming sick with worry. Perhaps Viktor was already on a plane to Russia and Lydia was lying dead and undiscovered somewhere. His mind was tormented with images, and the unfamiliar feeling of not knowing what to do scared him. Then a thought came to him; had Viktor drowned her?

As soon as the thought entered his mind he found himself running down to the shoreline. Of course she wouldn't be there, of course it was a waste of time and energy, but still he had to do it. He ran along the water's edge almost to Hove, then turned around and ran back. Perhaps he had missed something – some clue? But no, there was nothing.

He didn't know whether to be relieved or more worried – if that was even possible. He thought back to what Lydia told him about her intention to walk into the sea, and realised that if she was found dead on the beach, they'd assume she'd killed herself. With her mental history no one would question it. How long did a body take to show up? He didn't know the answer to this. Would it wash up on a beach miles away? Perhaps in another country, or far enough away so that no one would make the connection with the missing woman in Brighton. Then he would never know – or at least not for some time. This wasn't helping, worrying wouldn't bring results; he must do something.

Glancing at his watch, he realised he'd been hanging about on the beach for almost three hours, and perhaps something had happened at the shop; maybe she'd come back, maybe someone had found her. Realistically he knew they would have called if that was the case, but as he was thinking that his phone rang. It was Hannah and she was very upset. When he got her to slow down and tell him what the problem was, she told him she'd lost Angel. She explained that Angel whined and cried after Matt left, so Hannah had let her come into the shop as she thought she was probably lonely out the back. She seemed better, and settled down behind the counter, but as a customer came in she rushed for the door and was out before he could shut it. She told Matt she couldn't see any sign of Angel outside the shop and had no idea which way she'd gone. Hannah asked people if they'd seen her, but those who had didn't know which way she'd headed at the end of the street. She couldn't try to follow her as that would mean leaving the shop unattended and she'd no idea how to lock up.

Matt's heart sank; he couldn't lose Angel again. He owed it to Lydia to keep her safe, and if he lost her she would never forgive him. He realised that if he never found Lydia then she would never know; but he wouldn't allow himself to consider that possibility. He told Hannah he would come straight back, and once again he set off at a run. He was almost back at the shop when his phone rang, and a very irate lady told him that he wasn't taking very good care of his dog as she was once again sitting in the gardens outside her flat.

Matt was about to turn around and head back the way he'd come, but he thought he'd better let Hannah know first, so he stopped long enough to call her and tell her he was on his way to fetch Angel. Matt was exasperated, why did she keep going back to Bedford Square? If only she'd seen where Lydia had been taken, that would've been more useful. Hanging about where she used to live was no use to anyone.

Once again he broke into a run; the woman hadn't said she'd taken Angel in this time, so presumably it was possible the dog would disappear before he got there. When he arrived he went straight to the place in the garden where she'd been found before, but Angel wasn't there. He was about to go and knock on the woman's door when he spotted her. She was further up the square this time, close to where they used to live, sitting and staring at the old house. He walked up to her and bent down, but she didn't greet him; instead, she cried and whimpered, staring straight ahead. He was really worried she would pine away; she'd refused all food since Lydia had gone and now she wasn't even pleased to see him. He was about to pick her up, but she snapped at him, not close enough to connect, yet near enough to make him jump and step back. He couldn't believe this little dog would bite him, but understood how she must be feeling. He picked her up despite her growls and protestations, then walked across to look at the flat in daylight. He could see the window had been boarded up on the inside, so it was clearly abandoned. Perhaps it had been sold or the people who were renting it were going to do it up. Whatever the reason there was no sign of life there, and with Angel struggling in his arms and actually growling quite ferociously now, he thought he'd better get her home.

He didn't run back to the shop; he walked with a heavy heart. He couldn't put Angel down for fear of her running away again. Then he remembered that he had a lead. Feeling in his pocket he found the lead he'd picked up on the beach the night before. He quickly attached it to Angel's collar, and then with her beside him and unable to escape, he started to run. Angel had no option but to run with him.

When he arrived back at the shop, poor Hannah was overjoyed to see Angel and burst into tears. Matt felt terrible, he'd not given much thought to how Hannah was feeling, but of course she was as worried as he was.

'I thought she'd get run over or never come back, and how would I ever tell Lydia?' she said between sobs. Angel was unimpressed with her attempts to cuddle her and walked away from the proffered biscuit. 'Oh dear, she hates me now!'

Matt explained that she didn't hate her, she just wasn't interested in food and only wanted Lydia. He was becoming impatient; he had no time to deal with this. Hannah would have to pull herself together; the dog was back and he had to get on with his search.

What to do next, that was his big problem? He couldn't just wander backwards and forwards hoping to see her. He needed to think. Then he had a sudden brainwave: CCTV. There were cameras all along the seafront, most of the shops had their own, and the council definitely had several along the Kings Road. Surely at least one of them would have picked up something?

He decided to try the official line first, so he contacted the council, to be told they only had road safety cameras, and he would need to contact the police for the public safety cameras. Several more phone calls and much bureaucracy later he got precisely nowhere. Not only did the public not have access to the CCTV footage, but those that operated the system didn't take calls from the public either. He was told to put his enquiry in writing and given email contact addresses. By this time his patience was running out. He'd been inactive for too long; he was a man of action and he needed to do something more purposeful.

He made sure Angel was secured, and told Hannah not to worry – though he realised that would be of little help. Then he headed off to Kings Road to try to establish which private businesses had CCTV.

He felt bad about leaving Hannah again, but she was under strict instructions to keep Angel shut in the back of the shop and he really couldn't worry about either of them now. He was determined to find something this time but, as it turned out, the face to face enquiries proved no more successful than the telephone calls. All of the businesses he spoke to that did have CCTV either wiped their cameras on a daily basis or wouldn't have access to the recordings until the boss next came in. He wasn't sure they were all truthful, suspecting they couldn't be bothered to scroll through hours of film for Joe Public, so took the easier option and said they couldn't help. He was frustrated and angry, and faced the fact that, like it or not, he probably did now need the help of the police.

Chapter 22

It soon became light enough to see around the room. Viktor hadn't moved, and my assumption that he'd died seemed to be correct. Years ago, in one of my foster homes, I'd seen a dog die in a similar way. He was a collie of some sort, and in the short time I was there my loneliness drew me to him. I became quite fond of him, and he of me. I think he was quite old but he'd seemed in good health, although my foster parents said they thought he wasn't seeing very well. Then one evening he jumped up with blood pouring out of his nose and started fitting. I was sent up to bed, but the next day they told me he'd died and the vet said he had a brain tumour. Although I had no real idea, it wasn't beyond reason to conclude that was probably what Viktor had been suffering with too – which would also explain his delusions about Leo, and the terrible headaches.

So there I was, imprisoned with a dead man. Even though it was a horrible situation, I concluded it was marginally better than him being alive; although the thought of slowly starving to death amid the smell of a rotting corpse didn't sound like a great alternative. What could I do?

It was time for action. I couldn't do anything for myself trussed up like a chicken; my first priority was to get myself free. I'd managed to remove the blindfold the night before, but the next thing to tackle was the gag; at least then I would be able to make some noise. This was trickier than the blindfold, but at least I wasn't worried now about whether Viktor would wake and discover me doing it. The tape was stuck firmly to my face, and all I could do was scrape round the edges to try to get hold of an end to pull. I was making my face sore, but by holding my bound arms up, I could use both hands and eventually managed to peel back an edge to work on. There was no gentle way of doing it, and it hurt. My hands were too closely bound to allow me to rip it off quickly, so I had to endure the slow and painful peeling. Eventually it came off, leaving my face feeling as though I'd rolled in nettles. I could spit out the rags from my mouth and breath properly again. I almost wished I couldn't, as when I took a deep breath of fresh air I found it was anything but. The stench of Viktor had already pervaded the room, and with it came the nausea. I did not want to be sick there, where I couldn't get away from it, so I closed my mouth, breathed shallowly and refused to give in to it.

So now I could see and breathe, but I was still firmly bound. Both my arms and my legs were securely tied, with the latter still firmly attached to the radiator. I had nothing to cut the ropes with and I could see that Viktor had tied some pretty formidable looking knots. There was nothing for it; I would just have to use my teeth.

The enormity of my situation hit me. It would take hours to either untie or chew through the ropes on my arms, even if I could do it at all; and if I did manage it, I was still tied by my legs, Viktor decomposing all the while. I could try to make a noise to attract attention, and this would probably be my best option, however I couldn't rely on anyone hearing me or coming to my aid. I decided to start on the knots. I refused to die there.

After what seemed like hours of attacking the rope around my wrists with my teeth, I made little headway. The rope had shredded a little, and I certainly had a lot of it stuck in my teeth, yet nothing was any looser. I wondered if I should concentrate on the one around my ankles, although I would not be able to use my teeth on that. However, I reasoned that if I could get my legs untied I might be able to find something in the flat to free my arms. So, bent double, I set about the rope on my ankles, but realised with dismay that Viktor had fastened the knots on the back of my legs before attaching me to the radiator. No amount of twisting, turning and reaching brought them into my grasp. I cried with frustration and fear. I was never going to be able to free myself and no one would find me. I was going to die there alongside Viktor.

I sank back to the floor to rest and let my back unwind from its enforced folded position. I lay like that, puffing and despairing, aware of my pounding head, dry mouth and grumbling stomach. I was clearly dehydrated and in danger of becoming really ill. I must do something, and fast. I started to kick the radiator as much as my feet would allow, shouting for help at the top of my voice. But nothing happened.

At some point I must have fallen asleep, and when I opened my eyes it was dark, and the stench in the room was considerably worse. There was nothing I could do in the dark, but I started shouting and kicking the radiator again. As I was beginning to think there was no one left in the world, I heard a banging on the ceiling, and an aggressive male voice shouting.

'SHUT UP!'

Although the shout wasn't very friendly, at least it proved someone was in the building, so I continued banging and shouting in the hope that eventually they would do something. I thought my prayers had been answered when I heard someone open the gate and come down the basement steps. I started kicking my feet and shouting for help again, but my voice was hoarse and didn't carry, drowned out by banging on the door and the same male voice shouting.

'I don't know what you're doing in there, but if you don't stop the noise I'll report you to the landlord and get you evicted. And what's that awful smell, you filthy pigs?' With that he stomped back up the steps and clanged the gate shut.

It seemed there was no point shouting, or making

any kind of noise; no one would come, no one would help me.

I felt lightheaded and I'd lost track of the days; had I been here two days now? It was night again – was it only last night when Viktor died? Or was it the night before? I turned to look at the clock again to find it was 8 p.m., which meant I'd spent the whole day desperately trying to untie myself. Or had the clock stopped? I couldn't remember if I'd looked at the time earlier or not. Had it read the same time all day? Oh God, had it been 8 p.m. for days? I tried to stay calm; panicking wouldn't help. I would look at the clock again in a while to see if had moved. I wanted to take deep breaths but the smell was becoming unbearable.

Every part of my body was sore and stiff now, my mouth was dry, and bits of rope fibre were stuck between my teeth. I coughed to clear my throat and then couldn't stop, choking and rasping with no moisture to alleviate the tickle. When the spasm finally stopped and I was able to get my breath, my head was pounding and I wanted nothing more than to go to sleep. I no longer missed the soft mattress, the comfy pillow or the cosy duvet, and I was no longer aware of the cold. I was only aware of my exhaustion and the need for sleep, which came as soon as I laid back and closed my eyes.

***

The first thing I was aware of when I opened my eyes was the fly on my face. Brushing it away, I was also aware of the smell, and the number of flies in the room. It was light again now and I knew things were bad. The awful smell was making me want to retch, but my empty belly had nothing to bring up. Looking at the clock I was relieved to see it said 6 a.m., so it was working and this must be day three. I had to do something. Perhaps if I made enough noise the tenant upstairs would contact the landlord as he'd promised, but that could take days and I knew I didn't have days. I knew that if I didn't drink something soon I would be as dead as Viktor, and although I felt incredibly sick, I was also hungry. My body was desperately trying to survive and I had to join in the fight.

The time dragged on, no one else came, and I wasn't making much progress with the knots. Then, when I looked around again to check the time on the clock, I saw the can.

Why hadn't I noticed it before? I had been so intent on trying to discover if the clock was working that I hadn't seen it, but there it was, next to the upturned chair I'd been forced to sit on when I arrived. When Victor had attempted to rape me he'd put his beer down by the leg of the chair, and fortunately the can had remained upright, but unfortunately, out of my reach. Or was it? I put my arms above my head, even though my shoulder muscles protested. In this position I could just see the can over the top of my head and by stretching my fingers I could almost touch it. I knew if I knocked it over it could easily roll out of my reach, but I couldn't quite grasp it. I stretched my arms and fingers as far as I could, and my fingertips were less than a centimetre away from the can, but I could stretch no further. Frustrated and close to tears, I brought my arms back down and sat up. How could I get another centimetre closer? My back ached and my shoulders felt as if they'd been ripped from their sockets, yet I still couldn't reach. I shuffled back on my bottom and stretched my legs until the ropes bit through my jeans and into my legs, but I made no more progress. Then I had an idea; although my feet were firmly tied to the radiator, the ropes were round my lower calves, over jeans and socks which were rucked up under the ropes. If I could loosen the ropes maybe I could slip my legs through just enough to gain the tiny distance I needed.

I bent over and started to yank at the legs of my jeans, trying to pull them up towards my knees. To begin with

I made no headway, but as I pulled and gathered the material in my fingers the rope started to slip down to the top of my sock. Once I'd freed the jean leg from the rope I reached forward and started on the sock, this time pushing it down and pulling it out from under the rope. Before too long the rope was holding just my bare leg and it was definitely looser, so instead of being around my lower calf, it was around my ankle. I was triumphant, but exhausted, and took a breather before repeating the process on the other leg.

Once the rope was on both ankles I resumed my position on the floor and set about reaching for the can once again. The small difference had given me the distance I needed and I could finally reach it. I wasn't close enough to get my hand all the way around it, but could curl my fingers enough to move it towards me. Then just when I thought I had it, I felt it fall and start to roll, spilling the beer as it went. With lightning fast reaction, borne of desperation, I swung my arms across my body and grabbed it as it rolled past my head. I sat up with it clutched in my two bound hands feeling immensely proud of myself. I was laughing and crying as though I'd won an Olympic medal, yet in reality this was far more of an achievement. This could save my life.

Overcoming the revulsion of drinking from the same can as Viktor, and the awful taste of the warm, flat beer, I guzzled what was left in the can. It turned out to be most of it. Viktor had obviously hardly touched it, and the drop which spilled was minimal thanks to my quick reaction. The liquid and sugar content went some way to reviving me, even though it reminded me of my other pressing need. There was no point thinking about that, I would have to grip and bear it. As I drained the last drops from the can, I suddenly saw it for what else it was... a means of escape. If I could somehow break it open it would have sharp edges, and sharp edges would cut ropes.

Chapter 23

Matt was home again, and Hannah had left, promising to come back first thing in the morning. Angel was still refusing to eat. She had taken to howling now. Although Matt felt sorry for the dog, he didn't think he could take much more, and he decided to go out running again. It was dark, but that never worried him, and he knew he did his best thinking when he ran.

This time he didn't take his music, he wanted a clear head, and true to form he hadn't been out long when he started to think about Angel's behaviour. Why did she keep going back to Bedford Square? She must know by now that Lydia wasn't there. It would make more sense if she looked for her back at the shop, yet she ran away from there whenever she got the chance. He wondered how long scent lasted – did some part of the area still smell of Lydia? He'd seen some of the sniffer dogs working in Afghanistan and was amazed by their ability to find mines and explosives that had been buried far below the ground for a long time, so he knew dogs had amazing scenting ability. Yet unless Lydia had left something of hers behind he very much doubted if any of her scent would be there after so long.

So what on earth was Angel reacting to? Perhaps he should contact the landlord and find out if the flat was unoccupied, if he could perhaps take a look inside. Then he realised how absurd this would sound. *My dog can smell something, can I have a look?* No, he dismissed that idea almost as soon as he'd considered it. Yet it was strange about Angel. Whatever happened he couldn't risk her escaping and running back there again, or the woman down the road would be reporting him.

He realised the time had come to stop worrying about what the dog was doing and to report Lydia's disappearance to the police. It was over forty-eight hours since anyone had seen her, surely now the police would take the matter seriously? After trying and failing to view the CCTV, he knew the only way to discover if anything had been recorded was to go through the police – he probably should have done it sooner.

When he arrived back at the shop he found CM hanging around outside. Matt brought him inside and poured him a brandy, impatient to hear what he had to say. CM had arrived in Brighton earlier in the day with his two colleagues. He'd left them at the railway station to try to get access to the CCTV, while he'd checked out the hotels, hostels and even the rough sleepers in an attempt to track Viktor down. It was as though he'd arrived in Brighton and then disappeared, and despite spending some time enquiring at every type of temporary accommodation, there was no record of him staying anywhere. With MI5 authority his men had checked and rechecked the CCTV from the railway station. They reported that he'd definitely arrived in Brighton five days ago, and was seen getting off the train, but after that... nothing. They told CM there was no CCTV of him leaving the station and none on any of the cameras around the station area. However, CM was not satisfied and had insisted on seeing the footage for himself.

He told Matt that when he watched the film he noticed Viktor heading for the public toilets as soon as he got off the train, and this was then picked up by another camera trained on the entrance. It had taken a while, and a few pulled strings, but they'd managed to obtain a copy of this footage, and CM spent some time studying it. Sure enough he spotted Viktor coming out of the station, but not looking at all like the Viktor who got off the train. Instead of the overcoat he was wearing on the train he had on a blue quilted anorak and a black baseball cap. This appeared to have been enough to fool his men, but not CM with his fastidious attention to detail. Viktor was a slippery character, but CM had spent a great deal of time in surveillance and had no problem finding him. Once they knew what he looked like they followed him on various cameras. He headed towards the seafront, but there were fewer cameras there and the trail went cold.

Matt told CM that Viktor's route was not a surprise, as he probably wasn't sure if Lydia was still living at Bedford Square, which was just off the seafront, but that Matt had checked and the place was shut up and unoccupied. There were apparently no further sightings of Viktor Kolocov and no idea of where he went or what he did next.

None of this brought them any closer to finding Lydia, but what CM could tell him was that he was 100% sure Viktor Kolocov was still in the country and hadn't flown home, so this gave Matt some hope that at least she may still be alive. However, this thought brought him little comfort for, if she was, what was Viktor doing to her?

CM agreed that they ought to inform the police now, although he didn't tell Matt why he had come to this conclusion. Working on the worst case scenario, CM knew that if Lydia was found dead, the finger of suspicion would point at Matt, and if he'd not even reported her missing it would cement that suspicion.

Matt made the 101 call, and was told someone would be round to take the details, but was given no indication as to when this would happen. It seemed there was very little urgency or interest in starting a search for a missing girlfriend, and Matt did briefly wonder if the call taker would even deem it necessary to pass the details on. He realised that Lydia wouldn't be classed as particularly vulnerable, and as he'd told them nothing about Viktor or the threat, it wouldn't seem in any way urgent.

That done, Matt realised that reporting Lydia missing

by phone meant he would now have to stay at the shop until the 'someone' had been, which meant he couldn't go out and search, or even take the dog out. That wouldn't do; he was a man of action, and action, however futile, was what he needed now. He made a decision and told CM he was going to go to the police station and report Lydia missing in person. CM told him it was unlikely he'd be able to see anyone at the police station without an appointment; it wasn't possible to wander in and talk to a policeman on the front desk anymore. Everything was now done online or by phone. Nevertheless, Matt decided to take a chance on seeing someone at John Street police station, which was not far from The Lanes, and when he checked on his phone he found that it was open from 8 a.m. until midnight every day. CM realised there was no changing Matt's mind, so asked if he wanted him to go with him. Matt was grateful for the offer, but declined, saying goodbye to CM as politely as he could after arranging to speak to him again the following day.

As soon as he closed the door behind CM, he grabbed his rucksack with all the pieces of Lydia's phone in, shut Angel in the flat with a biscuit, and set off. It was just under a mile to John Street, where he was relieved to find all the lights on. However he was disappointed to find the main door locked, and was about to start banging and shouting when he spotted the telephone on the wall. He knew he must take himself in hand or he'd end up getting arrested. He picked up the phone and dialled the number as directed, took a few deep breaths and waited for a response. He realised he hadn't given them enough information in his earlier phone call, so it probably didn't set off any alarm bells, and this is what he explained to the man who answered. He also realised that sounding so vague and desperate may have appeared suspicious, but the voice told him to come to the main door and he would be let in.

A uniformed officer let him in, punched a code into

the inner door and took him through to a side room, this time accessed by an identity card around his neck. Matt, who was trained to assimilate and assess his surroundings at a glance, couldn't help noticing that this was an interview room and it was as though he was already a suspect. The room was characterless and square, with pale walls, an inaccessible window, and a single table and chairs in the centre. In addition there was a large mirror that almost covered one wall. He realised this was actually a one way window from where the proceedings in the room could be observed. The officer, who looked like a teenager to Matt, offered him a seat and a cup of tea or coffee and told him he would be back shortly. Matt took the seat but declined the drink, and wondered how long 'shortly' would be. There didn't seem to be any urgency, and despite the officer's smart and professional appearance Matt did wonder just how much experience he'd had.

He did in fact return in a very short while, which made Matt wonder where he'd been and who he'd spoken to, or had he just made a trip to the Gents? He sat down opposite Matt and took out his notebook, reinforcing Matt's feeling of being interviewed about a crime; all that was missing was the recording equipment. He introduced himself as PC Gary Lander and asked what had brought Matt to the station that evening – which Matt thought sounded like something straight from a TV show. So, in an effort to be taken seriously, he decided then and there to tell him everything. He told PC Lander Lydia's whole story from the beginning, as far as he knew it. He didn't hold back. He told the officer about the domestic abuse and subsequent killings, the suicide attempt and the return of Viktor, explaining his relationship to Leo, and the fact that he was a trained assassin. Out of necessity he showed the officer his MI5 credentials, which added some gravity to his statement, but from the moment he mentioned the killing of Leo and the baby the officer appeared to take things far more seriously. He told Matt he'd done the right thing by coming in, but he would need to take advice from a senior officer. Then he left the room. Matt resisted the urge to pace, but it took all his willpower to stay in his seat.

Then the door opened and PC Lander returned with a woman he introduced as Detective Inspector Hazel Spurgeon. As Matt shook hands with DI Spurgeon he was aware that the whole atmosphere had changed; it was clear the matter was really being taken very seriously now. The DI informed him that she had been involved in the case surrounding the deaths of Leo and the baby, and knew Lydia, albeit as a suspect. She told him that she'd felt very sympathetic towards Lydia at the time, although she wasn't the senior officer in the case, but had been relieved to hear the truth had come out and she'd been acquitted. She subsequently learned enough about Leo to take the threat from Viktor very seriously, but explained they must first examine all the less sinister possibilities. She would need details of Lydia's mobile phone, her bank details, and the names and addresses of any friends. When she mentioned the mobile phone it reminded Matt of the contents of his rucksack and he proceeded to empty it out on the desk. The officers exchanged glances; there seemed little doubt that Lydia had come to some harm. Matt told them he didn't have the information they needed with him, but he would gladly run back and get it. They told him there was no need, they would accompany him back to the shop, which he couldn't help thinking was to check it out. So they all left together and were soon inside a police car.

Matt knew it would actually have been quicker to run, as the car wouldn't be able to get close to the shop, whereas he would have cut through the side streets and been there sooner. However, he supposed he was still technically a suspect and they probably needed to keep an eye on him.

Once back at the shop Matt invited them in, and leaving them in the back room of the shop he went upstairs to Lydia's flat to find the details they needed. He felt as though he was invading her privacy, and he hated looking through her stuff. He managed to find her bank details and Hannah's address, as well as the name and address of her lecturer and the contact details for Sophie the social worker. Angel watched him in silence; there was no greeting, no wagging tail, just a cold, hard accusing stare. But when he went back downstairs she quietly followed him.

The officers made notes of all the details and told Matt to try not to worry; with her mental health history Lydia may well have had a breakdown and decided to run away. They assured him they would be doing everything in their power to find her, but Matt was really worried – did this mean they weren't taking the Viktor threat seriously? It was clear they didn't think Matt had done anything to her, as they were happy to leave him on his own – or perhaps this was just an opportunity for them to watch and see what he did next; a tactic he knew well from his surveillance work.

As they got up to leave, Matt felt the need to tell them Lydia wouldn't have gone without the dog, and foolish as this might have sounded to them, he felt it was a point he needed to make. He saw them out of the shop, and was just about to close and lock the door, when Angel streaked past him and was gone.

Matt chased after her. It was very late now, and although he didn't check the time he guessed it must be the early hours of the morning. He watched Angel disappearing into the distance, heading back in the direction of Bedford Square. Why? Why did she keep going back to a place that Lydia had left over six months ago? She wasn't a stupid dog, although she was in danger of being a dead one, for even if she managed to survive the run to Bedford Square it was almost three days since she'd eaten anything. Although he'd lost sight of her, Matt kept running, fairly sure of where he would find her. Sure enough, when he arrived at the square, there she was, silhouetted in the moonlight, looking every bit the Angel she was named for.

She was sitting at the top of the steps leading down to Lydia's old flat. She was trying to tell him something. As he approached, she rushed towards him, jumped up and wagged her tail, then turned, ran back to the top of the basement steps and gave two little yaps. Matt followed her and once again peered down into the dark. There wasn't a sound coming from the flat and no chink of light, but he made up his mind there and then that first thing in the morning he would call the agent and demand to look inside. If necessary he would use his MI5 identity and hint at terrorist activity; that should do it.

Despite her protests, he picked up Angel and began the walk back to the shop.

Chapter 24

It was no wonder my fingers were sore, as there were numerous cuts to the tips and plenty of blood. But they were nothing too serious, and I had made progress. I'd worked on the can for hours. I tried flattening it to begin with, but this proved too difficult with my hands tied together and no ability to move my feet; so I settled for twisting and bending it backwards and forwards until it started to split down the crease I made. Eventually, after much hard work, I ended up with two halves, and two very sharp edges.

I could have cried with joy, and for the first time since I'd arrived back at the flat I felt a surge of optimism, outweighing the awful smell and the flies buzzing around my head. I was going to get out of this place. I had no idea how long it would take, or how hard it would be, to saw through knots with the jagged edge of a beer can, but at least I believed it was possible. I'd spent so long thinking I was going to die and wondering when and how it would happen, that the relief I felt when the can broke in half was almost overwhelming. Now to get on with it and start living again.

I thought the obvious place to start was on the rope around my hands, as there was less to cut through than around my feet and and ankles, and once my hands were free I could possibly untie the knots around my legs.

I placed one half of the can on the floor for future use, while I figured out how best to use the other half. In order to cut the rope I needed to hold the can still somehow, and move my hands up and down so the rope ran across the sharp edge. The only way I could manage this was to grip the can in my teeth, yet here was the first problem. I couldn't open my mouth wide enough to hold the sharp edge vertically, which would be the most efficient option, so I had to hold it horizontally and turn my hands to the cutting position. In this position, with my hands up in front of my face, I couldn't clearly see what I was doing. Once or twice I misjudged it and cut my hands; luckily I avoided cutting my wrists.

It was a painfully slow process, and once or twice I felt like giving up. I had the added problem of the can bending if I put too much pressure on it, and then all I managed to do was turn the sharp edge up or down, leaving a crease which wouldn't cut anything. I had to keep taking the can out of my mouth so I could use my fingers to try to straighten it out again. This always resulted in more nicks and cuts, and my fingers were now very sore. Nevertheless, my survival instinct had returned. I wasn't going to give up; I would get this damned rope undone.

Over the next few hours I made some headway, but it wasn't helped by my constant dribbling from having the can in my mouth. I knew my body could ill afford this loss of fluid, but as each fibre parted I felt elated and even more hopeful of success. I changed tack every now and then and worked on my feet to give my mouth a rest, but didn't get very far.

Also, I knew the warm flat beer would only sustain me for so long, and I was becoming weak and tired now. It didn't help that it was getting dark again, and I realised I'd been working on the can for a whole day. I knew I'd have to get some rest or I'd collapse, so I lay my head on the floor, easing the pain in my back, and fell asleep immediately.

At some point in the night I dreamt I heard Angel barking, just two little yaps. I woke with tears in my eyes, remembering my little white dog. Whatever must she have felt when Viktor dropped her and kicked out at her? She'd never known anyone be anything but kind to her, and wouldn't understand what she'd done to deserve it. No wonder she'd run away. I drifted off to sleep again but this time there were no dreams, only a few hours relief from hell.

It was light when I opened my eyes, and all I could think of was food. For one blissful moment before I was fully awake, I wondered what to have for breakfast. Then the smell and the flies made my stomach heave and I remembered where I was and stopped thinking about food.

Yet everything was somehow better with the light. At least I could see the flies now and wave my arms at them before they settled on me. But there was no time to waste. I picked up the piece of can which I'd discarded the night before, and tried to decide on today's plan of action.

The previous day I'd alternated between my hands and my feet in order to make it easier on my mouth and my back, but the result of this was no great headway on either. I realised I'd not thought it through logically. If I could free my legs I would be able to search the flat for a knife or scissors, or anything else that would work better than a can, whereas if I managed to free my hands I would still be unable to move, and left with only the can and my battered fingers to free myself. So that was the new plan. Despite my back, which was screaming in agony, I would work on the ropes around my feet until they were loose, and then go in search of a better implement to free my hands. I decided the time had come to start using the other half of the can as I'd worn the first one almost smooth by my efforts so far. I fished around by my side where I'd carefully stashed it, and was amazed how much better it looked than the piece I'd been using.

***

At last. The final fibres binding my legs together pinged apart. I was free. I pulled my knees up, relieved to find they still worked. By this time the sun was streaming through the grilles, and as long as I kept my eyes averted from the grisly mound across the room then things looked decidedly better.

I wanted so much to live right then. I recalled my midnight trip to the beach all those months ago, and I couldn't believe how I'd almost thrown everything away – how I'd wanted to end the life which now felt dearer to me than anything.

First things first. A trip to the bathroom was top of the list, but getting up proved more difficult than I anticipated. My legs were weak and shaky and I couldn't use my hands to help me up while they were still tied in front of me. By rolling over onto my side and bringing my knees up I could use my elbows to get myself up onto my knees and forearms, and from there to a shaky stand. I wouldn't have to struggle to unfasten the waist of my jeans as they were already undone, thanks to Viktor. I rushed past his body to the bathroom, holding the front of my jeans so as not to trip. The relief was overwhelming. I knew in the circumstances it wouldn't have mattered if I hadn't made it, no one would have blamed me, yet I was pleased and proud I'd been spared that indignity. I felt slightly hysterical and giddy, and suddenly this made me laugh – as if anyone cared. Besides, no one was here, or likely to be. I could suddenly see the funny side of fretting about something so trivial, and that in itself made me feel good.

Feeling more comfortable, and in control, I knew I needed to find a means of freeing my hands. When I went into the kitchen area the first thing I saw on the worktop was a can of fly spray. That wouldn't help me get my hands free, but it would make the time spent doing it a lot less unpleasant. Grabbing the can in my tied hands, I turned around, walked back into the room, and let them have it. It gave me a vicious sense of satisfaction, and I used so much spray it made me cough and splutter, but it felt good to see them drop to the floor, buzzing and spinning. As I struggled to breathe I suddenly realised I could drink. There were taps; there was water! I dropped the can of fly spray and went to the sink. No point wrestling with cups or glasses; I turned on the tap and drank as if my life depended on it.

I found a suitable knife straight away; the carving knife from the kitchen drawer would do the job. But using a knife without free hands was a different thing altogether. I stood it on end in the drawer and shut the drawer so it would hold it, but as soon as I put any pressure on the blade it fell over. That wasn't going to work. I pushed against it into the corner of the drawer thinking it might work better, but it still fell over. I tried pressing my body against the knife as it stood on end in the drawer – however, it dug hard into me, so another failure.

Then I got a better idea. I got down on the floor again and wedged the knife between my knees. It took quite a bit of patience to get it right, and involved gripping the knife very hard, but I eventually got the hang of it and the ropes around my hands gave way. I was free!

I ran past the heap on the floor and reached the locked door. There was no key in the lock and no keys to be seen anywhere. I wanted to scream with disappointment; would I never be free? I didn't think I had the strength or the means to break down the door, so I turned to the window, ripping at the tape which held the curtains in place. I would smash the window; that would be my escape route. However, when I pulled the curtains open I could see this wouldn't work, as someone, most likely Viktor, had actually boarded the window up. It would have to be the door; I needed to find the key.

Then, as I raced around the flat, rummaging through cupboards, scanning the shelves, even combing every inch of the floor, I remembered. Not only had I seen Viktor lock the door, but also where he'd put the key. He had it on his person; I'd seen him slip it into one of his pockets. If I wanted to live I would have to search him.

Chapter 25

When Matt stirred from an uneasy sleep, he was filled with a feeling of doom. He hadn't gone up to the flat the night before; he couldn't face the emptiness of it. He'd made himself a drink downstairs and when he offered Angel some food she'd again refused. He worried that the little dog was going to fade away, but realised he hadn't eaten anything for days either, so perhaps they would starve to death together. He'd eventually settled in the chair to wait for the morning, and tiredness had overtaken him. His restless sleep lasted until the early light, and both his back and neck were now stiff and painful, so such sleep as he'd managed had been of little benefit.

Angel was lying by his feet, her eyes fixed on Matt as if willing him to do something. He'd made up his mind to go and see the flat owner this morning to try to obtain a key, but it was far too early yet. Perhaps he would go back there; he might be able to see something around the edges of the window. Looking down at the dog and her pleading face, he sensed this was the right thing to do, and he decided to take her with him.

After a quick shower for him and another refused meal for Angel, they set off, a man and his dog on a mission. Matt didn't know why he felt optimistic but there was something about Angel's demeanour that lifted his spirits, and as she trotted along beside him she looked as happy as she'd been since Lydia disappeared. He supposed she somehow knew she was heading back to where she wanted to be, but he had no idea why Bedford Square was so important to her.

It didn't take them long to arrive at the square, and Matt noticed that rather than trotting by his side as he was jogging, Angel had actually started to pull. When they entered the square there was no doubt where she was going, and when they got to the gate at the top of the steps Matt's blood ran cold. There was no mistaking the smell coming from the flat, it had drifted up the steps and met him full force as he descended. Any earlier optimism deserted him. He knew that smell; it was death. He was overwhelmed with fear, grief and rage, and without any hesitation he barged the door, and kept barging until he felt a slight give and a splintering sound.

***

I froze. I was about to brave the corpse and look for the key, yet as I crossed the room I could hear someone clattering down the steps and trying to break down the door. I called out, but my voice was hoarse and croaky.

The next few minutes were almost surreal; everything happened so fast, yet in yawning slow motion. The door creaked and splintered, a small gap appearing near the top before it burst open with a final loud crack. Then Matt was standing there in front of me, panting from exertion. Before I could take it in, a tiny white bundle came hurtling at me, yelping with joy.

I fell into Matt's arms crying and laughing, hardly able to stand. Then I suddenly found myself pointing at Viktor's body; it felt inexplicably important that I explained what had happened.

'I didn't kill him, he just died!'

***

The following hours were filled with blue lights and yellow coats, and I had the feeling I'd been there before, only this time I had someone to hold on to and my wonderful little dog to cuddle.

I was ushered out of the flat and up the steps, and

once again into an ambulance where a kind man looked me over and declared that – despite my appearance – there was nothing wrong with me that a meal, a bath and a good night's sleep wouldn't put right.

A female detective was giving the orders, and something about her was vaguely familiar, yet I was really too tired to care. Matt told her he was taking me home and she told her constable to drive us. She said she would need a statement, but it could wait until the following day; her priority for now was to deal with the body in the flat. Once again I was ushered into the back of a police car, and although the sense of déjà vu returned for a moment, I soon forgot everything other than the here and now. I rested my head on Matt's shoulder and let my eyes close, feeling the soft warmth of Angel in my lap. I was content.

Matt suggested we went back to his flat rather than the bookshop, as it had the luxury of a bath, and he told me I could have a long soak while he went to fetch anything I needed. When we arrived he made us both a cup of coffee and some toast, and found a tin of dog food in the cupboard which Angel almost inhaled in her rush to eat. I attacked my toast with the same fervour, and I couldn't remember anything ever tasting so good.

However, I was acutely aware of just how bad I must smell, and I loved Matt for not mentioning it. I asked if I could have the bath straight away and he went in and started running it. He apologised for the fact that his bath and shower gel both had a masculine fragrance, and I had the macabre thought that the live male smell was far preferable to the dead male aroma that clung to me – but I kept this thought to myself.

There was one thing I had to ask him though. 'Will you wait while I get undressed and take all my clothes away and dump them?'

'Yes of course, don't worry, I'll get rid of them for

you – and until I get back you can use my bathrobe. You'll also need a new phone and we'll get that sorted as soon as possible, but in the meantime you can use the landline if there's anyone you want to call.'

I couldn't help comparing him to Leo, who purposely dropped my phone in water and never replaced it, ensuring I could never phone anyone. This wonderful man was everything Leo wasn't.

I sat back down and made a list of everything I needed – just enough for a day or two and then I would go back to the flat. As Matt was about to set off he asked if he should take Angel with him for a walk. I told him I didn't mind, yet Angel clearly had other ideas. When she saw him pick up her lead she jumped on my lap and made it perfectly clear she wasn't going anywhere without me.

When Matt left, I went for my soak. The one thing about a near-death experience is that it makes you appreciate every little detail of being alive, and the bath was no exception. Hot and bubbly, albeit with Active Sport bubbles, and totally relaxing, I felt myself drifting off to sleep. Fearful of drowning I pulled myself up and started scrubbing. I wanted to ensure no trace of death clung to my skin, and using the shower head to wash my hair I eventually felt perfectly clean.

I got out of the bath and wrapped myself in Matt's lovely dark red towelling robe, then remembered I'd left a toothbrush here from my stay at Christmas, so was able to clean my teeth as well. I had no idea where to find a hairdryer, so I wrapped my hair in a towel and padded through to the bedroom in my bare feet and lay down on the bed.

I don't know how long I slept, but when I opened my eyes it was dark. There was a duvet pulled over me, and Angel lay next to me. It looked as though I'd slept all day. I jumped up like a guilty child and went through into the living room. Matt had nodded off in the chair with his headphones on, yet with some kind of sixth sense he woke up as soon as

I walked in.

My first night of freedom was marked with a Chinese takeaway, a glass of wine and a full night's sleep in the arms of the man I loved.

The following day I had to report to the police station and give my statement. I needn't have worried about it, as they were sympathetic and kind, and the whole thing was handled swiftly and efficiently. I was soon able to resume my previous life: moving back to my flat, resuming my course at uni and catching up with Hannah.

There'd been a report in the press, but nothing as sensational as when Leo died, and it didn't appear to stir much interest. So before long I was working back in the bookshop, with customers greeting me and asking if I'd been poorly.

Sometimes it was hard to remember what had happened over those three days. It was like a strange dream, or a crime I'd read about which had happened to someone else. But what I couldn't forget was how Angel never gave up on me. Matt told me how she kept going back to Bedford Square, and even snapped at him when he'd tried to take her home. It was her behaviour which finally convinced Matt to take a look and brought him to the door. So that was the second time she'd saved my life. Although Matt constantly reminded me that it was also my strength, presence of mind and resilience that played a great part in keeping me alive until they found me.

We agreed that although I'd been determined to stay alive, it was this little dog who'd kept fighting for me, who'd ensured I was saved; Angel by name and Angel in reality.

Chapter 26

The years passed by and our lives moved on. Matt and I married and moved into a lovely house in Rose Hill Terrace, with a beautiful garden which Angel really enjoyed.

I graduated and took up a teaching post at the Downs School, but this meant I wasn't able to give Matt any time in the bookshop. However, Hannah was still at uni and happy to have some work, and before long she moved into the flat. She is a teacher now, based at Bevendean, but she's remained at the flat and still helps out in the shop when she can. She's started a relationship with Darren, a PE teacher at the same school, so we often have them round for a meal and I think before long they will make it permanent.

I still see Amy from time to time, usually when she comes to Brighton for the reunions. We both go now, which I really enjoy. We occasionally meet up at other times of the year when she comes to The Lanes to shop – a habit Amy never relinquished despite living so far away, and something she always makes a point of doing at Christmas.

I've kept in touch with my foster parents, Terry and Sheila, and they are both very happy for me now that my life has turned out the way they always hoped.

In fact they are now foster grandparents, as I'm the proud mother of two little boys. They are my pride and joy, and together with Matt they complete the family I'd always dreamed of. Matt is still running our bookshop and also doing his extra work for MI5 from time to time. While the children are young and I'm not teaching, I'm able to cover for Matt, sometimes taking the boys with me. They love the shop anyway and so there is every hope of it staying a family business.

The only sad thing to happen in our lives was losing Angel well before her time. Two years ago she slipped away in her sleep, and both Matt and I were devastated. She wasn't suffering from any apparent illnesses, and the vet was mystified as to the cause of death. We will never know what happened and our only comfort was that she appeared to pass away without pain or trauma.

Nevertheless, my grief was overwhelming at first, and was accompanied by a certain degree of panic. I'd always believed Angel represented the new me, the strong me, and I wasn't sure I could be that strong without her. Neither Matt or I ever talked about replacing her, as to us she was irreplaceable, but when we went for walks there was something missing; that devastating sense of loss never went away. The boys kept asking for a puppy, and we faced the fact we'd probably have to give in at some point. Yet even the thought of getting a new dog always felt disloyal.

But the day I saw Angel again, everything changed.

I dropped the boys off for school and nursery one morning, and picked up the *Argus* on the way home. Although news is now readily available online, I've always enjoyed the tactile experience and visual clarity of a daily newspaper. When the children aren't around, I consider it my little luxury to sit with a cup of coffee and catch up with all the news. So that's exactly what I did when I arrived home that morning, and as I spread the paper out on the table, there she was!

Angel was on the front page of the *Argus* being cuddled by a little girl, under the headline "Little White Dog Finds Little Lost Girl".

Of course I knew it couldn't be Angel, but the likeness was uncanny and I started to read the story straight away. The girl had been picnicking with her family on the downs, before wandering off and becoming lost. There'd been search parties out well into the night, and she was discovered with a little white dog. The dog was sitting by her side and had been barking continuously to bring her rescuers to her. No one knew where the dog had come from, and she didn't appear to have any identification. She was only very young, not much more than a puppy, and had no microchip, so there was no way of finding out who owned her. The girl's parents were apparently so grateful they offered to give the dog a home, and it was clear from the photo she'd already formed a bond with the child. Apparently they wanted to call the dog Hero, but as it was a girl they settled for Star. The reporter then went on to make comparisons with "The Legend of the Little White Dog" which was apparently unique to Brighton. Several other places were known to have legends centred around a black dog, yet it seemed this was the only one that concerned a white dog.

I was amazed; I'd never heard this before, and although I wasn't born in Brighton I thought I'd been here long enough to have become acquainted with the local legends. Clearly not this one.

I looked at the photo again, but as it was a grainy print image it was hard to tell how close the resemblance was to Angel. I flipped open my laptop and quickly found the story and the photo on the newspaper's website. The beauty of the online image was that I could enlarge it on my screen, and as I did so, there was Angel, every tiny detail of her, including the eyes, which looked straight at me. I wanted her back; she belonged to me!

Then I realised how ridiculous that was. Angel had died two years ago, I had seen her dead in her bed, and I knew this couldn't be her. The pain in my heart was like losing her all over again.

I went back to the newspaper on the table. "The Legend of the Little White Dog" – I had to know more about this. I returned to my laptop and typed in the search box. There it was. There were a number of pictures: some grainy black and white ones, obviously from the 1940s and

50s, others taking the story right up to the end of the 20th century. All of the pictures showed the same little dog with various different people, and all the stories were about her turning up out of nowhere, exactly when she was needed, and staying for the rest of her life.

The stories were only brief outlines; I had to know more. Was my Angel this little girl's Star and all these other people's saviours too? I rang Matt at the shop and asked if there might be a book on the legend, gabbling on about what I'd discovered. He was fascinated and said he'd look into it and see if he could find anything out.

When he got home that evening he was clutching the book. I was amazed, but apparently not as surprised as he'd been when he'd found the book in the shop. He'd had no idea it was there, and he concluded it must have been bought in his aunt's time. Although he'd done a stocktake several times since taking over, he'd no recollection of ever seeing the book before, but when he went back in the old ledgers there it was, listed in his aunt's copperplate handwriting.

We pored over the book and did our best to share it with the boys. Some of the stories were about lost people, both on land and at sea, and some were about those attempting to take their own lives.

There was the man who sat on the edge of the Palace Pier trying to find the courage to let go, when a little white dog arrived and sat on his lap. He knew he couldn't jump without taking the dog with him. Then there was the whole family, saved from a house fire when they were woken by the little white dog barking outside their window.

It was so wonderful to read all these stories, to know our own small story was part of something much bigger. We felt happier thinking about Angel than we'd ever been in the two years since we lost her. We were convinced this was indeed her, the photos bore it out, and we'd been fortunate enough to share one of her several lives.

We understood that her return was our release; this was Angel setting us free, and even without discussing it we all knew we were ready for another dog to come into our lives.

Acknowledgements

I would like to thank Consuelo Rivera-Fuentes and Sophie Lloyd-Owen from Victorina Press who have made this journey so easy and exciting for me.

Also thank you to Amanda Huggins, whose advice and tips have made all the difference to this book, and to Triona Walsh for a brilliant cover design.

On a more personal note, thank you to my husband Paul for his support and belief, and last, but by no means least, to Ruby, my granddaughter, who persuaded me to write Angel after reading only my brief outline.

About the Author

Wendy Beasley writes hard-hitting women's fiction that keeps the reader in suspense, and *Angel* is her second novel in this genre. In contrast she has also published both fairy tales and dog books, and written a weekly column in the international magazine *Dog World* for over twenty years.

As a wife, mother and grandmother, her family are amazed and bemused in equal measure by this career change after many years in various administrative and secretarial roles, together with her hobby of high-level dog training competition. However, this is what has inspired Wendy's writing and ensured that any lack of formal qualifications are more than made up for by a lifetime of experience in love, conflict, relationships and rivalry, all of which are woven into her stories.